Stunned

Russell was supposed to f[...] Jackie in this romantic setti[...] [...]ed more interested in her sister, [...] 't fair, because Sharon already had a b[...] [...]d. A minor detail Sharon probably neglecte[...] to mention to Russell.

Jackie stopped abruptly, guarded from view by a veil of willow boughs.

Russell and Sharon were kissing. Not a sprightly little isn't-this-a-pretty-day peck, but a real kiss. A long, long kiss, too long to qualify for casual friendship.

Jackie was stunned.

Other Apple Paperbacks
by CANDICE F. RANSOM
you will enjoy:

My Sister, the Meanie

My Sister, the Creep

S—MY—
SISTER
—THE—
TRAITOR

Candice F. Ransom

AN
APPLE
PAPERBACK

SCHOLASTIC INC.
New York Toronto London Auckland Sydney

For my mother,
who should have had me first

ISBN 0-590-42528-X

12 11 10 9 8 7 6 5 4 3 2   0 1 2 3 4/9

Printed in the U.S.A.   28

Chapter 1

The summer following the Great Sister War promised to be one of the worst ever.

Jackie Howard sat on the well-cap in their front yard, glumly listening to her sister Sharon describe the perfect life, which neither of them would have, even if they lived to be a hundred.

Boredom stretched between the two girls like cobwebs. School had been out almost a month. There wasn't anything to do or anyplace to go or anyone to talk to except each other.

Jackie was glad her sister was around and not away for the summer like her friend Natalie, who was visiting her grandparents in Seattle. Sharon never said she was glad Jackie hadn't gone off like her boyfriend Mick, who was working as a camp counselor in the Blue Ridge mountains, but Jackie believed her sister was grateful for her company. Who else would listen to Sharon's rambling monologue of the perfect existence?

Central to Sharon's requirement for a perfect life was a car, ideally red and turbo-charged, but then cars had occupied a lofty position as a topic of conversation ever since Sharon had learned to drive.

"I'd hop in that car and head east without stopping," Sharon said now, wistfully watching the traffic cruise up and down Lee Highway.

"You'd run into the Atlantic Ocean," Jackie pointed out.

"West, then. Or south. It wouldn't matter, just so I got out of this hole."

Jackie's own desires were much fuzzier. A few weeks ago she had celebrated her thirteenth birthday, if you could call a birthday cake ineptly baked by Sharon and homemade chocolate ice cream so runny it had to be drunk through a straw a celebration.

Still, thirteen represented a magic number to Jackie. Back when Jackie was eleven and chafing with impatience to be a teenager like Sharon, she asked her mother when her life would get started, now that her childhood was officially over.

"Thirteen," her mother had answered.

Jackie had not been satisfied with the reply. "Thirteen! That's two whole years away! What about eleven? And twelve? If I'm not a kid anymore and I'm not a teenager yet, then what am I?"

Her mother had smiled. "Well, you could be a *tween*-ager. How's that?"

2

"I think it's stupid," Jackie scoffed. "Whoever made up the names for those numbers? It should be eleventeen and twelveteen so kids could know exactly what they are. None of this inbetween stuff."

"Be glad you have a few in-between years," her mother said. "When you get to be my age the numbers all sound alike as the years roll by faster and faster."

They weren't rolling by fast enough for Jackie, but deep down inside she knew her mother was right. She wouldn't be a real teenager until she was thirteen.

Now that she *was* thirteen, wonderful things should be happening to her, sort of like being allowed to buy clothes at a discount at Memco after showing your card at the door. She was breathlessly waiting for the glories of adulthood to shower upon her. So far, though, she hadn't seen a trace of a single solitary glory. Jackie doubted she'd even recognize a glory if one fell from the sky.

Instead, she faced a summer of sitting on the well-cap with her sister, watching the world go by.

Jackie traced the old powder burns in the cement top — "snakes" they'd set off on past Fourth of Julys. Maybe she was being unrealistic. Maybe expecting wonderful things to happen was too far-fetched, like hoping she'd wake up one day and look like her sister. Jackie and Sharon had the same coloring — brown eyes and brown hair. But Sharon was beautiful, with the fine, even features seen in oil paintings, whereas Jackie felt as if she'd been scribbled with a blunt crayon.

"Remember when we did these?" Jackie said, wishing she had a box of the slow-burning black pellets. She and Sharon used to see whose "snake," actually coils of ash, would be the longest. This year, of course, they were both too old for fireworks.

Sharon nodded. "We'd write our names with sparklers, too. You had trouble spelling yours."

"I did not," Jackie said, bristling a little. "It was just too long. The sparkler would fizzle out before I could print Jacqueline Howard."

"This summer is certainly a fizzle." Sharon drew up her knees and rested her chin on them. "I can't believe we're looking at the cars going up and down the road, just like we did years ago! Doesn't anything ever change around here?"

The Sister War had certainly changed things, at least for a while. The previous fall, Jackie had had a lot of problems with her older sister, whom Jackie thought was too mean for words. Then Sharon declared war on Jackie. The house was divided into separate territories, even the bathroom the girls shared, and they didn't speak to each other. The war finally ended when Jackie managed to bring Sharon and the boy she liked together.

"If one thing changed around this place, I'd faint," Sharon declared. "Just one!"

Across the highway, a man emerged from the side door of Nate's Garage. "Mr. Perkins changed his undershirt," Jackie observed with a giggle.

Sharon laughed, temporarily teased out of her bad mood. "It must be June," she added and they cracked up. Nathan Perkins, who operated the garage, wore what Jackie called "armhole" undershirts winter and summer, with dress slacks.

In summers past the garage provided a little drama when smashed cars were towed into the fenced area behind the building. Sometimes an argument between Mr. Perkins and an irate customer could be heard clear across the road and up the hill. When nothing was going on at the garage, Jackie would bet Sharon that the tenth car going toward Fairfax would be a blue station wagon or a white two-door, or whatever. Sharon made up fantasies about the people in the cars and the glamorous places they were going.

But they were beyond counting cars now, just as they were too old to set off fireworks.

Sharon said, dramatically pulling her hair, "If I don't get out of here, I'll go insane!"

"We can always go get the mail," Jackie suggested reasonably. "After the mail-truck comes."

"Yippee." Sharon's tone was acid with sarcasm.

"Well, it's *something* to do."

"I'm supposed to turn handsprings over getting the mail?"

"I can't help it that there's nothing to do!"

"I know," Sharon agreed, contrite. "I'm not blaming you. I can't afford to lose the only person close to my age within a forty-mile radius. We're so far from town. I despise living out in the sticks.''

This was an old complaint. Sharon griped continually about where they lived, a rural section of Fairfax County, Virginia. Washington, D. C. was only twenty-six miles to the east, but the city might as well be on the moon.

Before she started junior high, Jackie was perfectly content at home. Their brick rambler wasn't fancy, but the surrounding five acres the Howards owned consisted of a vast yard, a garden, and woods bordered on one side by a creek and on the other side by a rail fence that dated back to the Civil War. But the year before, when Jackie began seventh grade at Sidney Lanier Junior High, she understood her sister's grievance. Most of the kids who attended Lanier were from the suburbs, tightly-knit communities with tennis courts and swimming pools. Suburb kids hung out after school, instead of riding the bus home the way Jackie did. Living in a development, Jackie quickly discovered, was the key to having lots of friends.

''I had big plans this summer,'' Sharon muttered. ''First I was going to get a tan and then I planned to have a summer romance, like in the movies.''

''A summer romance? But you're going with Mick!'' Jackie couldn't believe her sister was considering being unfaithful to Mick Rowe, not after all Sharon had gone through to date him.

''Well, he's not around.'' Sharon wasn't even wearing Mick's class ring or the mustard-seed

6

necklace he had given Sharon for her sixteenth birthday. "I'm sure he's not pining for me. You know what they say, 'out of sight out of mind.' "

"I thought they said 'absence makes the heart grow fonder.' "

"That, too. It doesn't really matter. Mick's up in the mountains with a bunch of beautiful girl counselors in short-shorts while I sit here like a bump on a log. Even Linda has a job." Linda Taylor was Sharon's best friend.

"You could still get a tan."

Sharon lifted her long hair off her neck. "It's too hot. You can't get a good tan sweltering in the backyard. I need to be at the *pool*. Or the beach."

"How about if I spray you with the hose?" In the old days, before the summer of their discontent, they'd take turns spraying each other with the hose their father used for rinsing vegetables from his garden.

Sharon sighed. "It wouldn't be so bad living here if I could *drive*. I've had my license six whole months and Dad still won't let me take the car out by myself."

With a twig, Jackie stirred a doodlebug crater, a funnel of finely-ground silt, at the base of the well-cap. Her father once told her that if she called "Doodlebug, doodlebug, come out," nicely, the little bug would obligingly appear, but she found a twig worked better. This doodlebug crater was apparently vacant.

"I had plans, too," she said, snapping the twig in tiny pieces.

Sharon arched an eyebrow, a gesture she had

7

recently developed to make herself seem older than sixteen and a half. "You had plans? Like what? Fooling around with that club you and Natalie started in school?"

In seventh grade, Jackie and Natalie organized the Lanier Leopards, a club that was a huge success. But then school ended and the Leopards disbanded.

"No, that's over," Jackie said. "I kind of thought — well, things would happen to me when I became thirteen."

"What things?"

"You know, boys, parties . . . why isn't anything *happening*?"

Sharon snorted. "Don't expect miracles."

"You can talk. You already know how to dance, and you're on the drill team, and you've had at least five boyfriends." Jackie ticked off her sister's achievements.

"Yeah, but none of that came overnight, believe me. If reaching a certain age in life meant you'd get to do stuff, do you think I'd be sitting here? I'd be out in my own car, with the top down, looking for a cute summer boy."

"You've got a cute boy," Jackie insisted. "What's this summer romance business?"

"I'd just like to have one," Sharon said blithely. "The idea of a having a guy wild about me for just the summer sounds neat. In September, I'd go back to Mick." Her tone hardened again. "But how can I meet any boy stuck out here?"

Jackie thought it sounded underhanded to lead a boy on like that, cold-bloodedly planning

8

to ditch him at the end of the summer. Sharon was unconcerned because she was pretty and confident and opportunities were forever dropping in her lap. Jackie considered herself lucky to have a boy *look* at her for a few seconds. But what boy? Sharon's argument against living in the boonies, where the pickings were limited to Nathan Perkins in his undershirt and the flunkies who drove his tow trucks, had a lot of merit.

A breeze rustled the leaves of the big maple that shaded them from the hazy sun. Molehills heaved upward in miniature mountain ranges. The warmth soaked into the rough concrete of the well-cap, making Jackie drowsy. She could almost forget her problems.

"It's a conspiracy, you know," Sharon said suddenly.

Jackie roused herself. "What is?"

"The way our parents practically keep us prisoners from June till September. That's the main reason Mom and Dad won't let me use the car. They believe if they chain me to the house, I'll never grow up."

"You really think so?" Jackie had never examined her sister's situation in that light before.

"I know so. And what's more, it'll happen to you, too. They'll hold you back just like they're holding me back."

Jackie looked at her sister with new respect. Sometimes Sharon was so *deep*. Jackie just bopped through life, waiting for things to happen, but Sharon didn't take anything for granted. Sharon worried about more than not being allowed to drive — she had analyzed their parents' motives and arrived at a shocking conclusion.

By comparison, Jackie's own worries seemed trivial. This morning, for instance, she agonized over who would get the last Coke. She worried about it so much, she finally drank the Coke and hid the bottle behind the soap powder on the laundry porch.

Or sometimes at night when she couldn't sleep, she worried that the days ahead would all be the same, the way her reflection repeated endlessly when she gazed into two angled mirrors. Once, seeing Jackie mesmerized by the mirror trick, Sharon informed her she'd stumbled on the concept of infinity. Now her worry had a nametag, but that didn't erase her fears that her life would go on and on like the image in the mirrors with no change. Lying in bed, she tried to peer into her future, but couldn't see a thing. Was this because her parents were holding her back? If Sharon's theory were true, both their futures were at stake.

A rusty red Jeep stopped at their mailbox. A hand thrust a bundle of mail into the box and swiftly closed the lid, as if feeding an alligator.

Jackie stood up, glad for some diversion. "Mail's here! Race you down the hill!"

"I'm not running down the hill like a hoodlum for everyone to see me," Sharon said primly. "You go."

"Come with me. It's no fun by myself."

"You're only getting the *mail*, for heaven's sake."

"You just don't want anybody to see you without your makeup," Jackie said.

"I do not. It's — undignified to walk down that long dusty old driveway and have everybody stare at me. I'm only sitting here because we're so far back from the road, nobody can really see us."

Jackie scratched a mosquito bite. "I thought you liked having people stare at you."

"There's staring and then there's *staring*. I hate waiting for the bus right on the highway. People are always honking at me. It's so common, standing at the road."

"I guess," Jackie said. But she still thought her sister's prissiness was the prime motivating factor. Sharon wouldn't be caught dead at the Safeway unless she was wearing a sequined evening gown and tiara.

Jackie walked to the mailbox alone. The mail contained the usual assortment of bills, a letter from Aunt Geneva . . . and something else. She scanned the single sheet, then ran up the hill, whooping and waving the paper.

"Look at this!" she cried when she was close enough for Sharon to hear. "Now we know what they're building behind that fence down the road! It's an amusement park!"

Sharon snatched the circular. " 'Old Virginia City,' " she read out loud. " 'The frontier town of the East. Pony rides, cowboys, all the thrills of the Old West.' Oh, brother!" She wadded the paper and threw it on the ground.

"What's wrong with it?" Jackie demanded. "You wanted excitement! Here it is."

11

"A kiddie park is hardly what I had in mind." Slipping into her flip-flops, Sharon shuffled back into the house, presumably to mope in her room.

Jackie picked up the crumpled circular and smoothed it across the surface of the well-cap. Old Virginia City, the frontier town of the East. Okay, so it wasn't Disneyland. But the park just might be the wonderful thing she'd been waiting for since her thirteenth birthday.

It had to be better than counting cars.

Chapter 2

After supper, while her parents were busy working in the garden, Jackie went snooping.

Sharon started the tradition of nosing around when they had the house to themselves. Sometimes they'd snoop through their parents' dresser drawers. Or they'd root through their mother's jewelry chest. They never took anything, only fingered the onyx necklace and earring set their father had given their mother on their wedding day, or wondered why certain pictures had gained significance to be saved among the beads and pins.

Snooping made Jackie feel reassured, knowing the onyx set was always in the same place, along with Sharon's fifth-grade school picture and the tiny brass horseshoe a great-uncle had made for her mother when her mother was a little girl.

But tonight Jackie had a specific mission.

She couldn't stop thinking about what Sharon had said earlier. Suppose their parents really were trying to hold them back, make them stay children forever? What could they do about it? If she and Sharon came right out and accused them, their parents would only deny it. Grown-ups were sneaky that way. Unless she confronted them with proof.

Jackie dragged the white sewing bench from her mother's room, positioned it in front of the linen closet, and climbed up. On the very top shelf, behind the heating pad and a bunch of embroidered scarves, were two old sweater boxes. Grunting, Jackie tugged the boxes down. On the outside of one her mother had written, "This box is for Sharon." The other bore a similar label, "This box is for Jacqueline."

She pried the lid off her own box. It wasn't as full as Sharon's but it was getting there. Inside were report cards, Valentines, drawings, spelling tests, and other junk from school, like the stupid project she had done in third grade on transportation. She was amazed her mother saved such garbage. Smashing the lid back down, she took the boxes into Sharon's room.

Her sister was lying on her bed. Both the stereo and the TV were on, a measure of her boredom. The volume was turned down on the television so she could watch one and listen to the other at the same time. Sharon's black cat, Felix, was stretched out full-length on the windowsill, sniffing the gentle evening breeze.

Jackie lurched over a pair of high-heeled sandals. The county dump was tidier than Sharon's room.

"Have a nice trip?" Sharon said automatically.

"I'll be back in the fall," Jackie responded on cue. "What's on?"

"Some movie. What've you got?"

Jackie plopped Sharon's box beside her on the bed. "Remember what you said? About Mama and Daddy holding us back? Here's proof we're on to their little scheme. All we have to do is show them this."

Sharon raised herself on one elbow. "That's my school box. Put it back before I barf. The last thing I want to be reminded of is school."

Jackie fanned the sheaf of Sharon's report cards like a card hand. "Evidence," she said. "They are definitely trying to keep us kids forever. Why else would Mama keep this junk?"

"Mom's saving those papers so we can look through them when we're old like her and remember our school days." Sharon glanced at her report cards in disgust. "Though why she thinks we'll ever want to is beyond me." Sharon pulled out some sort of a chart. "Hey, I forgot about this. I did it for Mr. Hite's class."

"What is it?" Jackie tried to decipher the numbers in the crudely-drawn squares. Sharon's early schoolwork was even sloppier than hers.

"I was supposed to keep track of who washed up before supper. For hygiene." She pointed to Jackie's column. "According to my record, you never washed for one whole month."

Jackie frowned. She'd only been a little kid at

the time but Sharon's chart made it seem like she was the dirtiest child in Virginia. "How accurate is that thing?"

Sharon started snickering. "I copied it from the back of my health book! It's all a lie!"

"Well, one day when you're old like Mama you can look back at what a fraud you were in the fourth grade." From the "Jacqueline" box, she took out a yarn-tied booklet with crookedly pasted magazine pictures. "Look, I did this in Miss Boggs' room. Did you know that a camel is a form of transportation? And a bulldozer?"

Sharon said, laughing, "It's a wonder we ever made it as far as we have, looking at this stuff. I guess it's pretty nice of Mom to keep these for us."

Jackie put the lids on both boxes. "Then this isn't proof of their conspiracy against us?" she asked Sharon.

"No." Then she added, "But they're still holding me back. I can't drive the car, I can't get a job. I can't do anything."

Glancing around her sister's room, it was hard for Jackie to muster up much sympathy. Sharon had gotten new furniture the previous summer and Jackie received Sharon's scarred hand-me-downs. In addition to the stereo and the portable TV, Sharon owned a vanity table loaded with makeup, a million records, and a closet bulging with clothes. Tucked behind the vanity mirror was a blue-and-gray Fairfax High pennant. Sharon would be a senior this year and probably elected captain of the drill team as well. On another wall hung a poster that spelled her current boyfriend's name, "Mick Rowe," in letters snipped from newspaper headlines.

Next door, Jackie's room was practically a nursery, with her framed birth certificate hanging above her bed and her nature guides in the bookcase her father had made her. She didn't have new furniture or her own stereo or TV or a boyfriend.

"If you're being held back, then so am I," Jackie said, thinking of the adult privileges that had failed to materialize since her thirteenth birthday.

"Probably," Sharon allowed. "It's a little soon to tell, though."

Not to Jackie, it wasn't. A sudden inspiration made her sit up. "Sharon! You know what we ought to do — revolt!"

"You're already revolting."

"Be *serious*. We should fight for our independence, like our country did!"

Sharon seemed more interested than she'd been in days. "I think you've got something there. We really ought to stand up for our rights! A rebellion . . . not bad."

"The Sister Rebellion," Jackie clarified, thrilled her sister accepted her idea so readily. "We'll be like the Three Musketeers. Only with two of us."

Sharon grinned. "One for all and all for one!"

They shook hands to seal their alliance. Now things would happen! A terrific summer was just around the corner.

"I absolutely flat-out re*fuse* to wear that get-up where everybody can see me!" Sharon thrust the work shirt and broad brimmed straw hat into her mother's arms.

Mrs. Howard thrust them back. "If you don't put these on, the gnats will eat you alive. Hurry up, Sharon. I want to hoe the front garden before the sun gets too high. Jackie's ready."

"I'm not wearing mine, either." Jackie shrugged out of the old work shirt her mother had issued, like prison garb, she thought, and handed it to her mother. "It's too hot for that big shirt anyway."

The Sister Rebellion had begun. Jackie figured her sister was starting with a small protest, the way prison inmates in movies banged their tin cups to demand better food when what they really wanted was out. They'd gradually work up to bigger demands.

Even without the revolution as an excuse for not wearing those awful shirts, Sharon's reasoning made sense. It was entirely possible that one of Jackie's friends from school would drive down Lee Highway and see her dressed like a scarecrow. It might even be Daryl Forshay, a boy she had semi-liked the year before. "I thought that was Jackie Howard's house," he would say. "I didn't know peasants lived there."

Mrs. Howard tossed the hats and shirts on a kitchen chair. "All right, then. Let's go." She herded the girls outside and gave them each a hoe. They walked down the hill in the fresh morning air to the strip of garden that separated their front yard from the highway.

"Why doesn't Dad plant flowers down here?" Sharon grumbled. "The whole world knows we

18

grow our own corn and beans. It's embarrassing. Like we're too poor to afford food at the store."

"The best soil for corn and lima beans is down here," Mrs. Howard replied. "Besides, fresh vegetables taste a thousand times better than that processed stuff in the stores."

"But it's so *common*," Sharon persisted. "Crawling around in the dirt like a gopher."

"If I hear you say that word one more time I'm going to smack you," Mrs. Howard said.

"What word?"

"You know what word. Everything is common. Our house is common. This garden is common."

"It just means ordinary," Sharon said.

Mrs. Howard was not fooled. "Not the way you use it. Jackie, start on the row there. Sharon, you take the next row. With three of us working, it shouldn't take an hour to finish." She smiled. "If you girls help me today, we can all go to the the grand opening of that new park tomorrow night. Won't that be fun?"

"Tons." Sharon grabbed her hoe and began breaking up clods with a vengeance.

"Don't cut the roots," Mrs. Howard cautioned.

Jackie chopped the soil around the corn plants. It had rained two nights before and the red earth had baked like clay in the scorching sun. Hoeing was not her favorite activity. She was too short to hold the hoe right, and the handle kept whacking her on the chin. At the rate she was going, she'd be black and blue before she finished her row.

19

Sharon echoed Jackie's thoughts. "I despise this stupid garden. I don't know why Dad loves it so much."

"It's his pride and joy," Jackie agreed. Her father reveled in showing it off to visitors, who always exclaimed over the wondrous size of his tomatoes and the sweetness of his corn. People came from miles around to buy bushels of green beans and bags of beets, squash, and turnips.

Sharon swatted a swarm of gnats away from her head. "The gnats are murder."

"Maybe we should go back and get those hats."

Sharon stopped hoeing. She was farther down her row than Jackie, but not as far up as their mother. "My back hurts," she whined, loud enough for Mrs. Howard to hear.

"Don't bend so much," Mrs. Howard said helpfully. "You want to get a tan — gardening is a good way to get an even tan."

"I'd rather stay lily-white." Sharon hacked at a couple more dirt clumps, then paused again. "Hey, Mom! Want me to drive to the store? We're out of Cokes."

"We don't need Cokes," Mrs. Howard stated. "If you girls gobble up all the soft drinks before grocery day, that's your tough luck. Drink lemonade. Or water."

"Water!" Sharon gagged. "I'll die of thirst first. How about crackers? I noticed we're pretty low."

"There's a new box in the cupboard."

Sharon didn't give up easily. "You know, we don't have any melba toast in the house."

20

"Now there's a real necessity," Jackie said wryly.

"Be quiet!" said Sharon in an undertone. "I have an awful craving for melba toast, don't you, Mom?"

Mrs. Howard didn't look up. "Eat regular toast."

Jackie leaned on her hoe to stare at her sister. If this was a new strategy to further their cause, Sharon's logic eluded her.

"Wouldn't you like a piece of nice crisp melba toast with some of that special honey butter you make?" Sharon asked tantalizingly. "I could drive to the store in a jiffy, save you the trouble."

"You cannot drive the car unless your father or I are with you. That's the rule, Sharon. And I don't feel like changing my clothes to run up to the store. I've got a lot of work to do."

"But I'll get rusty if I don't drive every day!" Sharon wailed. "You and Dad work in this dumb garden until dark. When am I supposed to practice?"

"I'm sorry," Mrs. Howard said. "Maybe your father will let you drive to the park tomorrow night. But if you keep carrying on about it, he won't."

"If you let me use the car by myself just this once, I won't ask again," Sharon pleaded. "We won't tell him. I'll be real careful. I'll take up four parking spaces so nobody can dent the doors. Please, Mom. I'll hoe the rest of the garden for you, all of it. Please?"

Jackie felt sorry for her sister. Her parents were

really strict about Sharon's driving. Her father believed sixteen was too young to be out on the road alone, and he wouldn't give an inch.

Sharon hauled out the last of her ammunition. "I made straight A's in driver's ed! I was the best driver in my class!"

"The *only* class you made straight A's in, ever," Mrs. Howard pointed out. "Listen, Sharon. Even if you had degrees in driver's ed, and automobile engineering, and had a trophy from the Indy 500 to boot, it wouldn't do any good. Your father doesn't want you driving without him or me and that's that."

"No, it isn't!" Sharon flung down her hoe in a dramatic gesture, like Joan of Arc or some other famous heroine. "If you won't let me drive, then I quit!"

Mrs. Howard laid her own hoe between the rows and put her hands on her hips. "What do you mean, quit?"

"Just what I said!" Sharon yelled. "I'm sick and tired of grubbing in this hot, buggy, itchy old garden every summer! I don't eat the stuff, so why should I kill myself over it?"

"I never realized you were so near the brink of death," Mrs. Howard said. "If you don't eat anything from the garden, then how come you grab the first ear of corn before I get the bowl on the table?"

"Well, I'm not eating anymore! And I won't be a drudge anymore, either. I'm practically seventeen! Time people started treating me like an adult!" With that, Sharon stalked out of the garden, leaving her hoe behind for emphasis.

22

Envious, Jackie watched her sister march up the hill. Sharon's shoulders were squared, underscoring her vow that she wouldn't be back, ever. Then it occurred to her that Sharon had made the first strike for her independence. Was she supposed to quit, too? Maybe she should throw her hoe down and walk off like Sharon did.

Mrs. Howard said, "Don't get any ideas. We're going to finish these rows, you and I."

Reluctantly, Jackie resumed hoeing. It was too late to make her stand. She didn't have the nerve to defy her mother, and anyway, she liked corn and lima beans and other things from their garden.

"Don't forget we're going to Old Virginia City tomorrow night," her mother said breezily, trying to make light of the scene between her and Sharon. "That'll be fun."

"I bet Sharon won't go," Jackie said, knowing how determined Sharon was when she set her mind on a certain course. Having fired the first shot in the Sister Rebellion, Sharon wasn't about to retreat now.

"She'll go," said Mrs. Howard. "Sharon's still a member of this family whether she likes it or not."

Jackie scraped half-heartedly at the earth. Some rebel she was turning out to be, blowing the first opportunity to declare her independence. Sharon was probably taking a cool shower right this minute, free as a lark, while Jackie was just a gnat-bitten wimp, still firmly planted under her mother's thumb.

Chapter 3

"Sharon, does this look okay?" Jackie modeled her yellow skirt. "Or is it too dressy?" Before deciding on the skirt, she had put on white shorts and a rugby shirt and before *that*, cutoffs and a T-shirt.

Sharon barely glanced at Jackie, concentrating on her own image in her vanity mirror. "For heaven's sake, Jackie, we're not going to a coronation."

"I just want to look nice. Is that a crime?" Jackie noted that her sister was wearing *her* best shorts and a white sleeveless sweater.

"I don't even want to go to this stupid place. And I *wouldn't* go," Sharon said angrily, "except Dad said I had to. And he won't let me drive because I quit the garden. When I have kids I won't be so mean to them. The instant my kids turn sixteen, I'll buy them a brand-new car."

Jackie sat on her sister's bed, keenly interested. "Are you going to have kids?"

"Well, not this minute, but someday, after I get married." Sharon carefully applied a coat of her new summer lipstick, Teaberry. For someone who couldn't care less about the grand opening of Old Virginia City, Sharon was putting on enough makeup to qualify for the Miss America pageant.

"But you *know* you're going to get married and have kids?" Jackie pursued. "Even though you don't know *who* you'll marry?"

"Sure. Of course, I have a lot to do before then, like go to school and start my career, but I'm planning on marriage and a family." Sharon swiveled to face Jackie. "How come you're so concerned all of a sudden? Do you want my room that bad?"

Jackie was slated to move into Sharon's room after Sharon left home. "No," Jackie replied, although she had mentally rearranged Sharon's furniture to her own taste a few times. "It's just that I wondered how you know stuff like that — before it happens."

"Some things you just assume."

Easy for *her* to say. Sharon had already discarded more boys than Jackie had stammered hello to. Why was her future so murky while Sharon's seemed sharp as a postage stamp?

Sharon sighed. "Let's get it over with."

Mr. Howard was waiting in the car. "About time you people showed up. Tell your mother to come on," he told Jackie, irritated from the heat. "It never fails. We're all set to leave and

25

she goes back in the house to see if the iron is off." Jackie ran inside to urge her mother to hurry.

Before the car was out of the driveway, Sharon leaned forward and tapped her father's shoulder. "Dad, would you roll your window up?"

"Sharon, it's eighty-three degrees!"

"But my hair is blowing."

Mr. Howard rolled up his window. "Deliver me from a carload of females."

"I don't care if my hair blows, Daddy," Jackie said. "Short hair doesn't mess up like long hair." She didn't care if the wind snatched her bald-headed, just so she got to Old Virginia City. She'd read and re-read the circular until the paper was limp, still unable to believe a real-live amusement park was practically in her own backyard.

Since Old Virginia City was only a mile down Lee Highway, they arrived in minutes, churning up a cloud of dust as they parked beside the last car in the row. Jackie sprang out, nearly slamming the door into the side of the station wagon next to them. "Sharon, come *on*."

Sharon climbed out even more slowly than their parents. "This is so dumb. I can't believe I'm actually at a little kiddie park."

"It's not for little kids," Jackie corrected. "The flier said fun for all ages. Look at all the adults."

"Obviously they don't have anything better to do."

A man in a cowboy outfit took their money at the gate. "Have a rootin' tootin' good time," he exclaimed as he tore off a strip of tickets.

Sharon ducked her head, mortified. "If I see anybody here I know, I'll just die."

Jackie raced through the gate, giddy with excitement. The place was packed, which meant the park must be super!

Mrs. Howard caught up with them. "You girls stay together now. We'll meet you at that eating place over there in half an hour. Sharon, don't let Jackie get lost, you hear? We'll never find her in this crowd."

"Moth-er!" Jackie cried indignantly. "I'm not a baby!"

"You still get lost," her mother said. "Because you never pay any attention to where you're going. Sharon, here's some money in case you girls want a soda. Remember, the snack bar in half an — "

"All *right*." Sharon yanked Jackie down the main concourse, anxious to get away from her mother. "I'm surprised she didn't hire an armed guard to go on the rides with us."

"I'm surprised she didn't make you hold my hand. Where are the rides?" Jackie asked, glancing around.

Old Virginia City wasn't Jackie's idea of an amusement park. Wooden buildings flanked either side of the wide street — a church, a post office, a general store, Miss Rosita's boarding house — connected, like towns in wild west movies. At one end of the street were carnival-type games and a refreshment booth, at the other, kids clustered around a pony that was being led around a sawdust-covered track. Only the general store, the saloon, and an eating place called "Grub" were real, the others were facades.

"Is this *it*?" Jackie said, leaden with dismay.

Sharon yawned. "What did you expect?"

Actually, Jackie anticipated Old Virginia City to be a cross between Disneyland and *Gunsmoke*. Certainly more than a bunch of phony buildings tacked together and a pony ride. How could anything wonderful possibly happen to her *here*?

"Let's mosey on down to the general store." Sharon imitated the ticket-taker's western twang. "I'll buy you a cowboy hat."

"No thanks." Her excitement deflated, Jackie wanted only to go home.

Suddenly a man burst through the swinging doors of the saloon, rolling into the middle of the street like a tumbleweed. He was followed by another man wearing a tin star as big as a saucer. The marshal, or whoever, started to turn around when a boy yelled, "Watch out! He's gonna shoot!" The man on the ground had crawled to his feet and pulled his six-shooter from his holster. But the marshal fired first, low from the hip, the way the good guys did in the movies. The bad guy clutched his leg and went down like a water buffalo, bellowing in mock pain. A ferret-faced companion scurried out from behind a horse trough and helped the injured man limp away. Children stared slack-jawed. Adults applauded the actors.

"I bet they do that every hour," Sharon remarked. "Probably the high point of this place."

Jackie couldn't believe a staged gunfight was the pinnacle of entertainment. "This is so dumb," she said.

"I told you. Hey, is that Buddy Myers?" Sharon craned to see in the dispersing crowd.

"Who?"

"This guy from school. It *is* him. I'll be right back."

"I thought you said you'd die if you saw anybody you knew," Jackie reminded her.

"Buddy's cool. He's probably as bored as I am."

Jackie clutched the strap of her sister's purse. "Mama said we have to stay together." Sharon *would* see somebody she knew from school, a boy yet. If Jackie wasn't having fun, she didn't want Sharon to have any, either.

Sharon shrugged off Jackie's hand. "Don't be ridiculous. I'm only going right over there." She left Jackie to join a tall, blond-haired boy at the shooting gallery.

Alone, Jackie wandered down the concourse. Shrieking kids bumped into her, dribbling half-melted ice cream cones and purple slushee drinks on her yellow skirt. Some sported cowboy hats and bandannas purchased from the general store. They were having a great time. She would be, too, if she were five or six years younger. A group of teenagers Sharon's age congregated around the carnival games, whooping as they pitched baseballs for stuffed burros.

Jackie stood in the middle of the street. Pedestrians eddied around her as if she were a rock in a stream. She didn't belong anywhere in this place, too young for one end, too old for the other. She might as well go sit in the car.

Feeling exceedingly sorry for herself, she

scuffed her feet in the dust, the very picture of tragedy. If she projected her disappointment so other people could read it like a billboard, someone else might feel sorry for her. Maybe one of those cute high school boys by the ring-toss would come over and ask her what was the matter. Maybe take her into the saloon and order her a root beer. Probably even ask her out on a date. They'd go some place really neat, a zillion times better than crummy Old Virginia City.

But no cute boy stopped her and all she got for her trouble was gravel in her sandals.

Jackie sat down on the elevated wooden sidewalk in front of the post office to shake the pebbles out of her shoes.

"What are you doing wallowing around in the dirt?" Sharon demanded, bearing down on Jackie. "I told you to wait for me back there. I've been looking all over for you."

"I got tired standing in one spot," Jackie replied. "Where's that boy you were talking to?"

"Buddy? He had to get back to work. He runs the shooting gallery. He says Old Virginia City will clean up this summer and he's going to make a pile of money." Sharon's eyes shone at the prospect of making a pile of money. "The owner is still hiring. All I have to do is go talk to him, and he'll give me a job. Come on."

Jackie put her sandals back on. "Are we going to meet Mama and Daddy now?"

"Not yet. I have to talk to the owner first." Sharon darted through the crowd so fast Jackie could hardly keep up with her.

30

"Mama won't let you get a job. She said you're too young to work at night."

"According to her, I'm too young to cross the road by myself. Besides, this place is open in the daytime, too. I could get a day job." At the gate, Sharon made Jackie stay behind a hitching post. "I don't want him to think we're related. It's uncool to interview for a job with a kid sister tagging along."

"Thanks a lot." But Jackie let Sharon conduct her business with the owner of Old Virginia City, who turned out to be the ticket-taker.

When Sharon finished talking to the man in the cowboy suit, she was beaming. "I got the job!"

"Really? Doing what?"

"Working in the snack bar by the games. I'll be right next to Buddy. I start tomorrow evening. That gives me one whole day to convince Mom and Dad."

Jackie felt a twinge of jealousy. All Sharon had to do was walk up to the owner of the amusement park and she got a job, just like that. But then it occurred to Jackie that this might be good for the Sister Rebellion. Once Sharon's independence was launched, her own freedom couldn't be very far behind.

Since they were late meeting their parents, the girls hurried down the concourse into Grub. Mr. and Mrs. Howard had secured a table by a jukebox blaring country and western music. Mr. Howard wore a pained expression, as if his shoes were two sizes too small.

31

"Let's eat and get out of here," he said. "I've never seen so many kids in my life. If one more kid jabs me in the back with a toy six-gun — "

Mrs. Howard interrupted to ask him what he wanted to eat. Then she and Sharon stood in line at the counter.

For all the fancy western decorations, the restaurant was merely a glorified fast-food eatery. Jackie went over to the "fixin's" bar and filled little paper cups with catsup, mustard, onions, and relish. She bundled straws and plastic knives and forks in napkins and added packets of salt and pepper.

When she got back to the table, Sharon and her mother had returned with the food. Sharon's mouth was pinched with anger. Mrs. Howard dealt foil-wrapped hamburgers to each of them, her own face set in determined lines.

"What's the matter with you?" Jackie asked Sharon.

"She won't let me take that job." Sharon took a French fry and crammed it in her mouth.

Mr. Howard looked bewildered. "What's this about a job? How come I never know anything going on around here?"

"The man who owns the park offered Sharon a job in the snack bar. I don't want her working at night," Mrs. Howard replied, unwrapping Mr. Howard's hamburger and poking a straw into his Coke.

"It's not *real* late at night, Dad," Sharon said. "I'm off at nine-thirty."

"How are you going to get there?" Mrs. Howard asked.

32

"I could drive, if you and Dad ever let go of the car keys long enough."

"No driving," Mr. Howard said emphatically. "You're too young to be on the road by yourself. Young drivers just don't have the experience to judge situations and react."

"I'm too young to do anything except slave in that stupid garden!" Sharon retorted, pushing away her hamburger.

"If you won't work in the garden, you don't need to work anywhere else." Her mother smeared catsup on Mr. Howard's burger. He took the plastic knife from her before she could cut his meat for him.

"I'd like to know when I'm going to start living my own life, that's what I'd like to know," Sharon muttered furiously.

"I'd like to know when we're ever going to have a peaceful meal," Mr. Howard asked the empty air in front of him. "I've had heartburn for five straight years, since Sharon became a teenager."

"Jackie, eat your hamburger before it gets cold," Mrs. Howard admonished.

Jackie stared glumly at her hamburger, smothered in onions and mustard just the way she liked it. She wasn't hungry anymore. Everything was terrible! The amusement park turned out to be a dud. Sharon couldn't take the job she was offered.

The Rebellion was over before it had hardly begun. Jackie wouldn't gain her independence this summer or any other summer. Maybe it was just as well she couldn't see into her future.

Chapter 4

Jackie dumped more Sugar Crisp into the plastic margarine tub she used as a bowl. The second bowl of cereal in the milk remaining from the first bowl always tasted best. She could have poured the whole box and her mother wouldn't have noticed. Not the way she was arguing with Sharon.

"I thought we settled that job business last night," Mrs. Howard said.

"Well, we haven't. I don't know *why* you won't let me take the job." Sharon pounded the table with her fist so hard Jackie's spoon leaped right out of the bowl. "I could buy my own school clothes, my own groceries even. I could pay you and Dad board."

"The answer is no." Mrs. Howard carried her coffee cup to the table and sat down.

Jackie was glad Sharon had taken up the banner of the revolution again, even though it looked like a lost cause.

"But I'm in great demand!" Sharon cried. "I'm obviously dripping with talent, or Mr. Powell wouldn't have taken one look at me and hired me on the spot. Other kids fill out applications and wait months to get an interview and all I had to do was *stand* there. Doesn't that tell you anything?"

"It tells me you've let it go to your head," Mrs. Howard said. "Sharon, we have been over and *over* this. Your father and I don't want you working after dark."

"But there aren't any day jobs around here! All the day positions at the park are filled. There wouldn't be any jobs *period* if Mr. Powell hadn't built Old Virginia City."

Jackie spoke up. "Mama, I think you should let Sharon take the job." Her sister shouldn't have to fight alone.

"I think you should mind your own business," Mrs. Howard told her.

Sharon flashed Jackie a grateful glance. "Even Jackie knows you're being unfair."

Boldly, Jackie added, "If you were a government, Mama, you'd be overthrown."

Mrs. Howard didn't seem shattered by this profound observation. "You girls can gang up all you want. Sharon, you'll have the rest of your life to work. One day you'll thank me for letting you enjoy your summers."

"Enjoy!" Sharon said, indignantly. "I'd have

more fun at the dentist. How am I ever going to show my independence if you don't give me a *chance*? I'm sixteen and a half."

"You're a young sixteen." Mrs. Howard set her coffee cup in its saucer with a decisive clink, ending the discussion.

Sharon was far from through. "Sixteen is sixteen! I can't do anything around here. I can't drive the car because Dad's afraid I'll wreck it if I go more than two miles an hour. People give me jobs, and I can't take them. I wish I was never born."

"I'm having second thoughts myself," Mrs. Howard said with a gusty sigh. "And not for the first time."

Jackie remembered a time when she was about eight or nine. Sharon brought her friend Linda home from school one day, and they decided to devour a freshly-baked ham cooling on the back porch. Armed with forks, they dug the center out of the meat, too lazy to slice it. Linda went home and Mrs. Howard didn't discover the hollowed-out ham until supper time.

Sharon was blamed immediately — ruining a twenty-pound ham was exactly the sort of thing she'd do. An argument flared between Sharon and Mrs. Howard. Somehow Jackie found herself in Sharon's room with the door locked and their mother beating on the other side.

"Unlock that door this minute!" Mrs. Howard commanded, rattling the knob.

Sharon braced herself against the door, both thumbs pressed with all her might on the lock button.

Jackie wrung her hands. "We're really in for it now!"

"So who asked you to run in here with me?" Sharon said.

"Sharon, I'm telling your father when he gets home!" Mrs. Howard threatened. Eating the ham was bad enough, but locking the door was the worst offense. There was silence as Mrs. Howard worked the lock from the other side.

The tendons in Sharon's neck stood out from exertion. Her thumbs must have been killing her, Jackie thought, admiring her sister's tenacity.

"What's she doing?" Jackie whispered.

"I don't know," Sharon whispered back. "I don't hear her anymore. I bet she's gone for a bobby pin."

When threats failed — and they usually did with Sharon — Mrs. Howard resorted to a bobby pin to jimmy the lock.

Sure enough, they soon heard picking noises on their mother's side of the door. Sharon tightened her grip. She could even outlast the bobby pin.

"Jackie?" Mrs. Howard said piercingly. "Are you in there?"

"Don't say a word!" With one foot, Sharon blocked Jackie's access to the door.

Jackie whimpered. She knew what was coming.

Her mother's voice was authoritative, penetrating. "If you're in there, Jackie, you'll get it, too, when I unlock this door. But if you come out now, I won't tell your father."

"She's just saying that. She's using you to get

to me," Sharon said. "Mom won't do anything to you — she never does."

Actually, Mrs. Howard never did anything to Sharon, either. Their fights consisted mainly of yelling. Once in a while, Sharon would be grounded.

Buckling under the pressure, Jackie started to cry. She didn't want to be punished for what Sharon and Linda had done. "Let me out!" she sobbed.

Eyes flashing contempt, Sharon unlocked the door. "Get out, bawlbaby!"

She pushed Jackie out the door, and Mrs. Howard barged in. Sandwiched between her sister and her mother, Jackie felt the current of their tension travel through her body. In that instant, she realized Sharon's strong will matched their mother's. As Mrs. Howard stepped aside to let Jackie pass, Jackie detected a flicker in her mother's eyes. At the time she thought her mother was afraid of Sharon, which was ridiculous. Looking back, Jackie realized her mother was afraid of losing control over Sharon. That old fear had resurfaced now.

Sharon still clashed with their mother, only the methods and the nature of the arguments had changed. Sharon no longer bolted herself in her room and not just because Mr. Howard had removed the locks from the bedroom doors. Now Sharon hammered at her target with all the subtlety of a piledriver until she got what she wanted.

Dogging her mother's footsteps from the kitchen to the bedroom to the bathroom and back to the kitchen, Sharon harangued and wrangled ceaselessly about the job at Old Virginia City.

At last Mrs. Howard caved in. "All right! Take the job!"

Sharon won, but she had to meet Mrs. Howard's terms. She could only work a couple of hours in the early evening, after Mr. Howard got home from his job, and *she could not drive.* Her father would take her to Old Virginia City and pick her up. Sharon happily agreed to the conditions.

"I don't care if I have to ride in a wheelbarrow," she said to Jackie. "Just so I can have the job."

Jackie tooted an imaginary horn. "Victory for the Sister Rebellion!" After Sharon's triumph, surely it was her turn next.

The first evening, Jackie and her parents dropped Sharon off at Old Virginia City and then went to High's for ice cream. It was very pleasant sitting in the parking lot. Jackie put her feet up on Sharon's side of the seat and leisurely ate a Nutty Buddy she didn't have to share with her sister, who always took such big licks Jackie hardly had anything left by the time she wrestled her cone back. She rolled both windows down all the way. Her parents talked about buying a new brand of fertilizer, while Jackie daydreamed about the exciting possibilities waiting for her this summer.

When they picked Sharon up at nine-thirty, Jackie saw her sister by the gate, laughing with a group of teenagers, mostly boys. Sharon told them she'd see them tomorrow, then ran to the car. She threw herself in the back seat like a sack of coal, exclaiming, "I'm soooo tired! You would not believe how tired I am!"

"I don't want to hear it," Mr. Howard said to Sharon. "You pitched a fit over this job, and you're going to stick with it till the end of summer. That's what independence is all about."

"Oh, I don't want to quit," Sharon said hastily. "I love it. You meet such interesting people in the work world."

"Yes, I saw all those interesting people you met." Mr. Howard tried to catch Sharon's eye in the rearview mirror, but Sharon pretended to look in the other direction.

At home, Jackie went into her sister's room. Sharon lay across her bed like a plank.

"So, what's it like to be on your own out in the world?" Jackie asked eagerly. "Did you flirt with boys the whole evening?"

Sharon groaned. "Hardly. I filled five hundred milion paper cups with ice. Put another five hundred million frozen pretzels in this special oven. Cleaned the soda machine." She rolled over and sat up. "I didn't talk to the other kids until I got off duty. Working is the pits!"

"Are you going back?"

"I have to. If I said I didn't like it after all I went through, Mom would never let me hear the end of it." Sharon massaged the small of her back.

"But look what you've done for our cause," Jackie pointed out. "You have a job!"

Sharon flopped down again. "Lucky me."

"It's my turn now," Jackie reminded her sister.
"Your turn for what?"

"You know, to be independent like you." Had Sharon forgotten their agreement: One for all and all for one?

"You can have *my* job, if you're dying to be independent."

Jackie had something more fun in mind than work. But Sharon was clearly too wiped out to be of much help that night. Maybe tomorrow they'd begin campaigning for Jackie's freedom.

"It probably won't be so bad tomorrow," she told her sister.

Sharon sighed. "I hope so. If the Egyptians built the pyramids, I guess I can make a few billion pretzels."

The next day Sharon slept practically the whole afternoon, until it was time to get ready for work. When she came home that night, she told Jackie she hadn't felt compelled to toil every single second and liked her job a lot better. Linda called and Sharon talked to her until after Jackie went to bed. The third night, Sharon didn't complain at all, describing the neat guys who visited her booth. They never did get around to Jackie's problem.

Jackie found that going to High's for ice cream wasn't quite so much fun anymore. The evenings were long and draggy without Sharon.

Then came payday.

Sharon made a very big deal of going into the bank to cash her first paycheck. In the car, she took her money out of the little brown envelope and counted it four times, laying the bills on the seat between her and Jackie. Jackie could have memorized the serial numbers.

"What are you going to buy?" Jackie asked, hoping Sharon would offer to take her to the movies to celebrate their victory.

"A new wardrobe," Sharon replied immediately, as though she'd been forced to wear rags her entire life.

"You don't have enough to buy a new wardrobe. But you've got enough to . . . um, go to the movies and maybe treat one other deserving person," Jackie hinted broadly.

Sharon didn't even hear her. "This is only my first paycheck. I'll get this amount every week. I can buy all sorts of things."

Saturday Sharon went shopping. She bought herself a white skirt and a pink top, both on sale, and had money left over for a pair of sunglasses. Simmering with envy, Jackie calculated how many outfits Sharon would be able to buy until school began in September. She wasn't supposed to feel jealous of her sister. They were working toward the same goal. Sharon had just gotten there first. Still, Jackie wondered when *she* would reap a few benefits from the Sister Rebellion.

While Sharon was getting dressed one evening, Jackie sprawled on her sister's bed, playing fingers-under-the-covers with Felix. "It's my turn," she said.

Sharon adjusted the waistband of her new skirt. "You've said that before but you haven't told me *what* you want to do. You might as well forget about getting a job or learning to drive. You're way too young."

"But I want to be grown-up, like you!" Jackie blinked back tears. She was too old to cry, though she felt like crying more than ever these days. "We had a deal! I helped you, now you have to help me."

"What did you do for me?"

Her sister had an awfully short memory. "I took up for you when you and Mama were arguing. I said she should let you have the job."

"Yes, you did," Sharon acknowledged. "And I appreciate it. But, Jackie, you can't just lie there and tell me you want to be independent. *How* do you want to be independent?"

"I want to have fun. Dances and parties . . . maybe even a boyfriend." All things Sharon was doing when *she* was thirteen.

"I don't blame you," said Sharon. "But we need to start slow. I'll have to work on Mom."

"When?" Jackie pressed. "Tomorrow?" Time was dribbling away. Summer was more than half over.

Sharon suddenly adopted a lordly manner. "We'll see." That was what their mother always said when she had no intention of saying yes, but wanted to postpone the screaming and yelling. With her sunglasses perched jauntily on her head, Sharon left for Old Virginia City.

Jackie and her parents drove straight home. No ice cream that night. Jackie roamed aimlessly around the yard, feeling abandoned. Lingering twilight only served to make the days seem endless. Fireflies emerged from the grape vines, flashing against the dark green leaves like Christmas lights. Jackie kept seeing her sister in her new white skirt and sunglasses, skipping off to her fascinating job. Sharon's summer had taken off like a rocket, while Jackie's wasn't even worth mentioning. Since she'd got what *she* wanted, Sharon had conveniently forgotten the rest of the cause, helping Jackie.

A lightning bug zigzagged past her. Jackie reached out and captured the firefly gently in her hand. The lightning bug's tiny feet tickled her palm. Her cupped hand lit up briefly, the creases of her fingers outlined in red.

When she was little, she used to catch fireflies and put them in a mason jar with holes punched in the lid. Back then, her summers had been jampacked with fun. She collected bird's nests, made rock villages by the creek, wove clover chains. Summer was her own special kingdom, which she ruled by the light of a firefly lantern.

But now she was too old to build fairy houses, too young to get a job. If this summer was a preview of life after her thirteenth birthday, she might as well have stayed twelve.

Jackie opened her hand, disillusioned by her thoughts. The stunned lightning bug hesitated, then flew off winking into the night. Even a firefly had something to do, someplace to go.

Chapter 5

"The eighth listener who calls in — "

Jackie didn't even wait for the radio announcer to finish his sentence before rapidly dialing the number of the radio station. A busy signal blatted in her ear. She slammed the receiver down and dialed again. Busy. Dialed again. Still busy. She switched off the radio on the telephone table, annoyed.

"What do you keep slamming the phone down for?" Sharon asked, coming into the hall.

"It's busy," Jackie said crossly. Lately Sharon had been too caught up in her own affairs to give her the time of day, much less help Jackie gain her independence. "No matter how many times I call WPGC, I get a busy signal. I'll never win an album." A thought struck her. "Maybe if I called at three in the morning — "

45

"I've tried it. The line's always busy, even in the middle of the night."

It figured. Even if all Jackie had to do was dial a number, she'd never be the eighth caller of the hour or the fourteenth or the twenty-third.

Sharon twirled the phone cord. "Suppose you did reach the deejay, you'd be too shy to yell out the radio slogan, so you still wouldn't win the album."

"I would, too," Jackie said hotly. "I know the slogan by heart."

"I know you *know* it. I said you'd be too shy to say it on the air. You can barely answer the phone here." Sharon raised her voice to mimic her sister. " 'Mama, the phone's ringing. Do I have to answer it? What'll I say? I mean, after hello, what do I say?' "

Jackie winced inwardly. She *did* have trouble answering the phone. She hated the way the phone could ring any old time, demanding to be answered. Whoever was calling knew he was calling the Howard residence but *she* had no idea who it was and the thought made her tongue-tied. In two seconds the person on the other end would find out how dumb she really was. Once she told a man selling aluminum siding that her mother couldn't come to the phone because she was in the bottle. She had meant to say "in the bathroom," which was almost as bad, but in the grip of phone paralysis "bathroom" came out as "bottle."

"I don't think that's funny," Jackie said.

"It *isn't* funny," Sharon agreed. "It's pathetic. You can't even order pizza."

"Yes, I can. I just don't want to . . . right now."

"Jackie, if you don't nip this phone shyness in the bud, you'll never make it in high school." Sharon should know, having spent most of her waking hours attached to the phone. "If you want to be independent, you'd better start now. Do you want Mom answering the phone for you when you're thirty?"

"No."

"All right, then. Talking on the phone is like everything else — it's just practice. Make a lot of calls, dozens of them."

Jackie didn't quite follow Sharon's train of thought. "You want me to order a dozen pizzas?"

"No, you need to *call* people to cure yourself of this shyness." Sharon had evidently appointed herself an expert on the subject of telephone jitters.

"You mean like call up a store and say 'Do you have Prince Albert in a can?' "

"That's kid stuff. I mean a real call."

Jackie thought about who she'd like to talk to. Natalie. But she was in Seattle. Her mother would die if a call to Seattle showed up on the phone bill. Besides, Jackie didn't know Natalie's grandmother's number. "I could always talk to the president," she joked. At least he wasn't long distance.

Sharon was flipping through the phone book.

"Are you looking up the number of the White House?" Jackie asked incredulously.

"I'm looking up the request line to WPGC. You're going to request a song."

Jackie's blood chilled, even in the July heat. "They put requests on the air, Sharon."

"I know. It'll be good practice." She marked the place with her finger. "What song do you want to hear?"

"One with not too many words in the title," Jackie said, remembering the bathroom/bottle mix-up.

"How about 'Yesterday'?"

"They probably won't have an old record like that," Jackie said, stalling.

"They'll have it." Sharon began dialing the radio station.

"Wait!" Jackie stopped her sister in mid-dial. "What do I say?"

"You say 'Is this the request line? Could you please play 'Yesterday'? Okay, I'm dialing again." She passed the receiver to Jackie. "It's ringing."

A surge of panic nearly knocked Jackie flat. This is nothing, she told herself. People phoned requests to radio stations all the time. Even knowing *she* was the one to initiate the call, and therefore had the upper hand, did little to calm her fluttery insides. "They're not answering." She started to give the phone back to Sharon when she heard a click on the wire. Someone had answered.

"Is this the request line?" she whispered faintly. Her heartbeat pounded in her eardrums. What was she supposed to say next?

"Ask them to please play 'Yesterday,'" Sharon coached. "And speak up!"

"Ask them to please play . . . I mean, could you pease pay . . . I mean, PLEASE PLAY . . . uh — "

"Give me that." Sharon snatched the phone. "They hung up. No wonder. Honestly, Jackie, all you had to say was a simple little sentence!"

"Well, who could concentrate with you right in my face? You made me nervous." A poor defense but the only one she had at the moment.

"If talking on the phone makes you nervous, how will you ever survive these dances and parties you want to go to? It'll only get worse," Sharon said gravely. "First it's the phone, then it'll be making friends at school. Boys don't like shy girls. You want to get asked out, don't you?"

"Yes, but what does that have to do with calling radio stations? It's my turn to rebel and be independent. You promised to help me." Was Sharon going back on their agreement?

"I am," Sharon insisted. "You have to take it one step at a time. How do you think guys will ask you out? On the *phone*."

"But I want to go out *now*," Jackie wailed. "I'm tired of waiting!"

"Jackie, you don't know anybody to go out *with*." Sharon considered a moment. "Maybe we can use your problem to get you out tonight."

"To a party?" Jackie perked up. Now this was more like it! "How? What are you going to do?"

"Trust me," Sharon said, striding into the kitchen where their mother was putting away

49

the supper dishes. "Mom," Sharon announced. "Did you know Jackie's social skills are non-existent?"

"Is that right?" Mrs. Howard said absently.

"Yes," Sharon replied. "And it's serious. Jackie's too isolated. She needs to socialize with other kids. I think she should come with me to the park tonight. Mr. Powell lets family members of the employees have free admission."

Jackie slumped with disappointment. Old Virginia City! She wanted to go to a *party* . . . or out on a date.

Mrs. Howard did not jump at the suggestion. "I don't know. Who's going to watch her? You'll be busy in the booth."

"Watch her? See?" Sharon asked no one in particular. "This is the very thing I'm talking about. Mom, Jackie is *thirteen*. She doesn't need anybody to watch her."

"She's young for her age," Mrs. Howard maintained.

"I am not," Jackie protested. Sharon was right — her mother *was* holding her back.

Sharon took Jackie by the shoulders. "Look at her, Mom. She's hopelessly backward. She can't even call a *radio* show. If she doesn't get out, she'll be a reject all her life!"

"She goes out . . . she rides with Daddy almost every night to pick you up," Mrs. Howard said, wiping the stove.

"That doesn't count. She doesn't meet any *people*. She has trouble making friends in school because during the summer she reverts back to her geeky awkward self."

Jackie wriggled out of her sister's grasp. "I am not backward and geeky! Just because I fouled up one lousy phone call — "

Sharon gave her a warning kick. "This is part of my plan," she whispered tersely. Louder she said, "Mom, you can't keep Jackie a baby forever. If you hold her back, she'll never come out of her shell. She's not like me."

"And you think hanging around Old Virginia City will help Jackie socially?" Mrs. Howard asked Sharon.

"I know it will."

Didn't she have a say in this? Jackie didn't even *want* to go to Old Virginia City. She'd had her fill of that one-horse town the night of the grand opening. There was nothing there for her — the park was geared for little kids or kids Sharon's age. But mostly, she resented Sharon and her mother haggling over her life — *her life* — and how she should spend it. Sharon might be trying to help her, but Jackie questioned her sister's tactics. Labeling her a reject and bossing her around . . . whose side was Sharon on anyway?

"I don't want to go," Jackie declared.

"You see?" Sharon said to Mrs. Howard. "She's too chicken to go to an *amusement* park."

"I'm not chicken! I just don't want to go!"

Mrs. Howard eyed Jackie as if she were a laboratory specimen. "Maybe you do spend too much time by yourself, especially since Sharon's working. Ask your father. If he says it's okay, you can go with Sharon tonight."

"But I don't — "

51

Sharon elbowed Jackie in the ribs. "You want to sit home forever? Ask Dad quick then go get ready. He'll say yes. He always does."

Old Virginia City wasn't as packed as it had been on opening night. Kids still dodged slower-paced grown-ups, but the crowd was definitely thinner.

In her refreshment booth, Sharon tied an apron over her skirt and pinned a little frilled cap like a paper cupcake on her head.

"Meet me here in about an hour," she instructed Jackie. "Most of the mob will be gone by then, and I have a break. We'll go visit Buddy."

Jackie had no idea how she would occupy herself for five minutes, much less an hour.

The phony gunfight was in progress in front of the saloon. Jackie sidled by goggle-eyed children and wandered toward the main attraction at the far end of the park, the pony ride.

She stopped at a wide board fence that prevented people from straying into the sawdust enclosure. A gray pony grazed behind a barn. A little girl astride a honey-colored pony squealed with delight as the animal was led around the ring. The girl's parents waved encouragingly from the sidelines. The young man leading the pony had his back to Jackie as he completed the circuit. When the ride was over, the young man swung the little girl from the saddle and set her down.

The boy turned around and faced her. Jackie

drew in an astonished gasp, as though a mule had kicked her in the stomach.

He was positively gorgeous. Tanned from hours outdoors, tall and lean, like a real cowboy. Up till then, Jackie's standards of boys were measured by the Daryl Forshay Scale, judgments based on the boy she sort of liked in seventh grade. One look at this guy and the needle jerked off the chart, blowing a gasket in Jackie's system.

The boy approached the fence, towing the pony. "Hi. I'm afraid you're too old to ride Ginger," he said, his blue eyes teasing. "Your legs would drag on the ground."

Jackie felt herself blush to her toenails and hoped the boy thought she had a heat rash or something. "I was just . . . uh . . . noticing how the ponies really seem to like you."

"Oh, my sweethearts are crazy about me," he said, but not in a bragging manner. "I treat 'em good, give 'em sugar, keep their stalls nice and clean. Cookie and Ginger are great animals to work with, very easy-going."

"Did you train these ponies?" Jackie asked, not the least tongue-tied. Was it possible a real cowboy worked in a rinky-dink place like Old Virginia City?

"Not me. It takes hours and hours to break wild ponies. But I went to Chincoteague for Pony Penning Day once. Those little guys can really swim!"

Jackie nodded. She had read *Misty of Chincoteague* and knew about the island off the coast of Virginia where the wild ponies were rounded up every July and herded across the channel to the next island to be auctioned. "It seems kind of mean, doesn't it, making the ponies leave their home."

"It's the only way to keep their population down. Otherwise, the ponies would run out of food and starve."

"I suppose you're right."

Ginger poked her head over the top rail and nuzzled Jackie's neck. "She wants you to pet her," the boy said.

Jackie stroked the velvety nose. "She's adorable. I'd love to take her home!"

Laughing, the boy fished a lump of sugar out of his pocket. "Feed her this. She'll follow you to the ends of the earth. You love yummies, don't you, Ginger-baby?"

Jackie held her palm up. The pony took the sugar from her, delicately, as if her hand were a platter of the finest china. "She's so mannerly."

"Actually, Ginger doesn't like just anybody. You must be pretty special for her to take up with you like that." The boy ruffled Ginger's shaggy mane affectionately. "Can you get the pretty girl to tell us her name?" he asked the pony.

Jackie giggled, blushing again. He thought she was pretty! She could die happy! "It's Jackie. Jackie Howard. Well, it's really Jacqueline, but everybody calls me Jackie."

"I'm Russell Bass. Pleased to make your acquaintance," he said formally, like the sheriff meeting the school marm. "Is this your first time at Old Virginia City?"

"No, I've been here before," she replied. "My sister works in the refreshment stand up by the shooting gallery. I'm just hanging around till she gets off work."

"Well, I'm sure glad you came down here. You've brightened our day, hasn't she, Ginger?" Then he added, "What's your sister's name? Maybe I've met her."

"Sharon."

"Sharon Howard," Russell said to himself. "Nope, doesn't ring a bell."

"Believe me, if you'd met Sharon, you'd remember."

"If she's anything like you, you're right, I wouldn't forget her." He glanced over at the turnstile where another tiny customer clutched his ticket. "Ginger and I have to get back to work. See you around sometime?"

"Well . . . I don't know," she stammered.

"Come back. Promise?" He led Ginger onto the sawdust track. "Bye."

Suddenly Jackie felt sweaty behind the knees. He wanted her to come back! Russell Bass, the handsomest boy she had ever seen in her entire life!

Her heart soared like a kite. The wonderful thing she'd been waiting for had finally happened! And what was even more amazing, Russell Bass was clearly interested in *her*. Hadn't he asked her — begged her, really — to visit him again?

Jackie gazed longingly at the fenced-in pony ring. To think she hadn't wanted to come. Now she never wanted to leave.

Chapter 6

On the way home, in the privacy of the dark back seat, Jackie half-leaned out the open window, letting the soft summer wind rush past her. She imagined she looked very romantic. If only Russell Bass could see her now, her hair streaming out behind her (even though it was short, her hair *felt* like it was streaming), a mysterious smile curving her lips. His heart would catch and he'd think, *Never before have I seen such a breathtakingly beautiful girl. . . .*

"Jackie! Can you hear me?" Mrs. Howard twisted around in the front seat and touched Jackie on the arm. "Get inside this car. Do you want an earache?"

Reluctantly, Jackie withdrew from rushing romantic thoughts to the ordinariness of the car. Even in the dark, she sensed her sister staring at her.

"What are you, an Irish setter?" Sharon remarked.

"Just enjoying the night air," Jackie said blissfully.

Mrs. Howard half-turned in the seat again. "Did you have a good time, Jackie? Sharon, did she behave?"

Jackie hated it when her mother did that, ask her one question, then ask Sharon practically the same question, as if Jackie was too dense to answer for herself.

"I didn't even see her most of the night," Sharon said. "She went off and didn't come back until right before closing."

Once she met Russell Bass, Jackie lost all track of time. She watched him lead Ginger until the pony ride shut down for the evening. From a safe distance away, of course. As much as she wanted, she couldn't go back to the fence and drool. It would have been too obvious, as if she were chasing him. When the lights along the main concourse dimmed to indicate the park was closing, she realized with a jolt that she hadn't checked in with Sharon for nearly three hours. She ran down the concourse to the other end, where Sharon was talking to her friend Buddy Myers.

Sharon looked worried. "I was about to send out a search party. I couldn't even find you on my break. Where've you *been*?"

"Umm . . . around," Jackie replied evasively.

Sharon had two pretzels wrapped in a napkin. "These were left over. Are you hungry?"

Jackie was starving. She would have killed for

a hot pretzel slathered with tangy mustard. But suppose Russell came along and saw her wolfing down a big fat pretzel, maybe with mustard on her chin? "I'll eat it later," she told Sharon.

At nine-thirty on the dot, their parents drove into the parking lot. Mrs. Howard examined Jackie to make sure that on her own she hadn't suffered any ill effects.

Now Mrs. Howard asked Jackie, "So what did you do all that time?"

"I watched the people." Well, she did. One person, anyway.

Their car turned into the driveway, crunching gravel under the tires. Were they home already? Jackie was still too keyed up to go in the house. She went around back to the patio and stretched out in the lounging chair, arranging her skirt so the pleats draped prettily around her legs, like a lady in a perfume ad. If Russell saw her lying in the purpling shadows, he'd whisk her off to some romantic foreign country. Some place where roses bloomed year-round and the sun never stopped shining because people in love shouldn't have to look at ugly stuff.

The kitchen window was just above the patio. Jackie could hear the clatter of spoons and the wham of the silverware drawer as her mother fixed her father a snack. A rectangle of butter yellow light from the window slid down the brick wall to the edge of the patio, just missing Jackie. Under the protective cover of darkness, her thoughts drifted to Russell.

He was so handsome, and so nice. For some

reason, she didn't feel shy around him. If he called her up, she'd even be able to talk on the phone with him. She just had to see him again!

Her mother's voice floated out to her. "Where is Jackie? Jackie, are you out there?"

Jackie sat up, her pose ruined, the dreamlike mood shattered. "Yes!"

"Come on in. It's time for bed. Daddy wants to lock up."

Honestly. How could she do something as mundane as go to bed on the night she had fallen in love? Of course her parents didn't know, couldn't know, or she'd never be permitted to return to Old Virginia City. With a sigh, Jackie went inside.

Sharon's light was still on. Jackie hesitated at her sister's door. If she wanted to see Russell Bass again, she'd need Sharon's help.

Sharon was writing on a pad. She glanced at Jackie. "I thought you were in bed."

"Not yet. Are you writing to Mick?" asked Jackie.

"No."

"Oh. I thought you might be. You promised to write him every day when he left for camp." Jackie knelt to pet Felix, but the cat slinked out of reach. Snooty animal.

"He hasn't written to me since he left. Why should I waste my time writing him?" Sharon said.

"He's your boyfriend, not mine." If she had a guy away at camp, she'd write him twenty-page letters every single night. Funny thing about Sharon — she went to great lengths to snare her boyfriends, but made little effort to keep them.

Jackie recalled the time Sharon entered the ninth-grade science fair at the last minute, because a boy she liked had also entered. On the night of the fair, the family got dressed up and drove to the high school. Jackie was amazed at the fabulous entries, barometers and botany projects, a scale model of our solar system, and a real working carburetor. And there was Sharon's project — a shabby old poster of a volcano she'd whipped up an hour before the event. Jackie could have done better herself blindfolded, and she was only in the fifth grade. Sharon's was the worst project in the whole fair, but she didn't care. Jackie could still hear her mother's indignation.

"Sharon Howard, you drag us out here for a poster you didn't spend two minutes on and all these other kids have made wonderful projects!"

Sharon wasn't upset. She'd never had any intention of winning, entering the fair was only a way to flirt with this boy. After the science fair guy asked Sharon to go steady, she went with him for a while, then threw him over for a basketball player. Her sister was hard to figure.

"These are the clothes I want to put on layaway," Sharon said, holding up the pad. "But I won't have enough money to get them out before next June, much less September. I wish I earned more." She stared at Jackie. "Are you okay? You look sort of strange."

Jackie flew to Sharon's vanity mirror. Girls in

love were supposed to be radiant. Her face didn't look radiant, more wind-burned than anything. And her hair was snarled from hanging out the car window.

"Do you have something to tell me?" Sharon asked her.

Jackie bit her lip. If she told Sharon she'd met a guy and had to see him again, Sharon would probably volunteer a lot of unwanted advice. Granted, her sister had loads of experience with boys. But this was *her* first love, and she didn't want Sharon directing her every little move. Still, Sharon was her passport into Old Virginia City.

"I just . . . wanted to say thanks," Jackie mumbled.

"For what?"

"For taking me with you tonight. If you hadn't talked Mom into letting me go, I wouldn't have — " She stopped, on the verge of blurting out her encounter with Russell Bass.

"Wouldn't have what?" Sharon pumped.

"I wouldn't have . . . uh, mingled with other people, like you told me I should. It was good for me. I'm glad you're helping me . . . not be held back," she finished lamely.

"That's the whole object of the Sister Rebellion," Sharon said.

In an effort to sound nonchalant, Jackie's voice came out an octave too high. "Do you think Mama will let me go with you again tomorrow night? I mean, one night of mingling isn't enough. I need lots of practice, like with the phone."

Sharon frowned. "Two nights in a row . . . I

doubt it. You know how Mom is about letting you do stuff by yourself."

"What about the next night? Or Friday night?" If she didn't see Russell soon, she would *perish*.

"All right! I'll ask."

Jackie nearly dropped to her knees in gratitude. "Thanks, Sharon. I really appreciate it."

"Don't get your hopes up."

Her hopes were already aiming for Mars. She was in *love*, for heaven's sake.

Jackie went into her own room and undressed for bed. Unable to sleep, she scooted down to the foot of her bed and rested her elbows on her windowsill.

After a few seconds, her eyes became accustomed to the dark. The tall poplars and oaks marking the woods beyond the back garden came into focus. Squinting, she made out two images in the black leafy treetops, a poodle dancing on its hind feet and a lady in a poufy bonnet. She'd discovered the tree pictures years before. They were always there, the dancing poodle and the lady in the bonnet, part of the summer landscape.

Jackie whispered Russell's name, her lips close to the window screen. Releasing his name in the moonwashed night gave her back the summer powers she thought were gone forever. She shivered with delight, remembering the hiding place she had when she was eight.

Her old hiding place was actually a roll of fencing wire next to her father's cucumber patch, outfitted with a canvas floor mat. On lazy summer afternoons, Jackie would crawl inside on the sun-warmed canvas and read Sharon's old Nancy Drew books. Weeds growing around the wire trapped moisture and the canvas gave off a moldy, nose tickling scent. Jackie loved lying in her hideout, breathing in the heavy summer aroma, the cucumbers slumbering in the sun nearby.

Being in love, she decided, was like being back in her hiding place. A warm, fragrant secret all her own.

As Sharon predicted, Mrs. Howard wouldn't let Jackie accompany her sister to work the next night. "You can ride with your father when he picks Sharon up," her mother said, and Jackie had to be content with that. She counted the seconds until it was time to leave for Old Virginia City.

They arrived ten minutes early. Jackie bolted from the car, on the pretense of going to meet Sharon. Once inside the gate, she raced down the main concourse, not even pausing at Sharon's refreshment booth, to the far end.

Russell was removing Cookie's halter. He saw her and flashed his brilliant smile. "Hey there, Jackie."

"Hi!" Jackie clung to the fence, jiggling the lowest board with her foot. She was so nervous!

"What have you been up to?"

"Nothing much. Is Ginger okay? How come you're using Cookie?" she said. The ponies were teriffic conversation-starters.

"I rotate them," he replied. "Ginger worked the day shift so Cookie did the evening shift."

He tipped his hat back. "Though Cookie only gave five rides tonight. So, how've you been?"

"Fine." Her heart skidded against her rib cage. He was so gorgeous and so sweet, asking about her. If only she had more time!

"I still don't think I've run into your sister," Russell said. "The concession people high-tail it out of here at nine-thirty on the button but I have to stay and groom the ponies."

"What time is it?" Jackie asked desperately.

"Nine-thirty-three. Do you have an appointment?"

She bounced off the fence. "I've got to go. My sister will kill me if I'm late. Bye!"

"Come again when you can stay longer," he called after her.

Her sister had already closed her booth for the night when Jackie ran up, panting. "I went out to the car," Sharon said, "and Dad told me you came in to get me. Where have you been?"

"Nowhere in particular." But Jackie suspected her sister wouldn't buy the same excuse tonight.

"You have too been somewhere. You're acting weird again. Now tell!"

Maybe it was time to let Sharon in on her secret. After all, the whole purpose behind their alliance was to help each other that summer. "I met this boy yesterday," Jackie said, the words tumbling out. "He runs the pony ride. I think he's a real cowboy. I . . . kind of like him."

"A boy!" Sharon shrieked. "I should have guessed. And he runs the pony ride? What's his name?"

"Russell Bass." How she loved saying his

name out loud, instead of merely whispering it into the night!

"I don't think I've seen him around," said Sharon musingly. "I have to meet the guy who has you running all over the park like a maniac."

"You can't meet him without me!" Jackie cried. Russell was *hers*, she saw him first.

"I'll get off five minutes early tomorrow night. Business hasn't been that hot lately so Mr. Powell shouldn't mind. Then we'll go see your cowboy." Sharon pushed her toward the gate. "We'd better hurry before Dad comes in after us."

"Can I borrow your mustard-seed necklace?" Jackie asked Sharon the next evening.

Her sister was getting dressed for work. "If you promise not to lose it. It was my birthday present from Mick, you know."

Jackie fastened the fragile chain around her neck. The glass magnifying ball containing the tiny seed dangled in the hollow of her collarbone. The mustard seed was a symbol of faithfulness. After Sharon met Russell and satisfied her curiosity and then got lost, Jackie would be alone with Russell. He'd probably comment on the necklace. She'd tell him the legend and it would only be natural for Russell to admit his love for her.

The three hours of Sharon's shift seemed interminable. At last it was time to go get her. Mr. Howard waited in the car, listening to the radio. Jackie set a new world's record as she vaulted into the amusement park.

"I bet I didn't sell a dozen pretzels," Sharon reported as they headed for the pony ride.

"There he is!" Jackie said, her voice trembling. Russell was leading Ginger to her stall.

"So that's Wonder Boy." Sharon fluffed her hair and pasted on a big smile.

Russell came over when he spied the two girls. "Hey there, Jackie. Who's your friend?"

"My sister. The one I told you about? Sharon, this is Russell. Russell, this is my sister Sharon."

A grin slowly spread across Russell's tanned face. "Jackie said if I ever met you, I wouldn't forget it. She was right."

Sharon gave that tinkling little laugh she used whenever a boy was within a fifty mile radius. "I ought to complain to Mr. Powell — keeping a real cowboy way down here where nobody can see him."

"Funny, but I've suddenly developed a craving for pretzels," Russell said. "I'll have to come up to your stand at least seven or eight times a day."

They laughed and looked deeply into each other's eyes.

Jackie felt herself fade into the background. Russell never noticed the mustard-seed necklace she was wearing or anything else about her. Why should he, with her beautiful sister there?

Chapter 7

Jackie cornered Sharon in the bathroom as soon as they got home. Sharon was brushing her teeth, using too much toothpaste as usual. She looked like a rabid dog, but she didn't look one tenth as mad as Jackie felt.

"You had to do it, didn't you?" Jackie accused immediately.

"Do what?" Sharon asked around a mouthful of foam.

"Smile at Russell like you did. You know, that girly smile you put on around boys."

"For heaven's sake, Jackie, all I did was say hi. What did you want me to do, bite him?"

"I want you to leave Russell Bass alone! He's mine!"

Sharon rinsed her mouth under the running tap instead of drinking from the glass. As she dried her face on the towel, she said, "What are you getting so steamed about? I didn't *do* anything."

Jackie hopped up and down like Rumpelstiltskin when the miller's daughter guessed his name. "I saw him first! You have no right to act gooey around him. You've got a boyfriend. Russell is mine."

"He is?"

"Well, he will be." Jackie would probably be going steady with Russell right this minute if Sharon hadn't demanded to meet him. Once he saw Sharon, he was a goner.

"Jackie, Russell Bass is at least eighteen. He's much too old for you." Sharon grimaced in the mirror, baring her teeth to inspect her gums.

Jackie hated her sister's teeth. They were even and perfect, the square front teeth like Chiclets. Jackie's own front teeth overlapped slightly, something she was terribly self-conscious about these days. She thought her teeth gave her a rabbity appearance, whereas Sharon smiling at herself in the mirror resembled a mouthwash advertisement. It simply wasn't fair, the way Mother Nature rewarded her sister with the best of everything, while Jackie wound up with the dregs.

And now Sharon was about to snatch the *one* boy Jackie knew was meant for her.

"I won't have it!" she said, stamping her foot.

"Won't have what?" Sharon tore her gaze from her reflection.

"You can*not* have Russell Bass. I know you, Sharon. You were making eyes at him." The expression was their mother's, corny and old-fashioned, but that was exactly what Sharon had done, flirted at Russell with her eyes.

"He is cute," Sharon allowed, straightening the towel on the rack with exaggerated care. "In fact, he's the cutest guy I've seen this summer. Lots cuter than Buddy. Or even Mick, when you get down to it."

"I was right! You *are* planning to make a move on Russell, aren't you?" What could she do about it? Since her sister and Russell worked at the same place, Sharon would have plenty of opportunity. And pitted against Sharon's physical attributes, Jackie felt very puny indeed. Still, Russell was technically hers, and she wasn't going to give him up without a fight.

She narrowed her eyes at her sister. "We'll just see who Russell likes best."

Sharon laughed, infuriating Jackie even more. "Is that a challenge, little sister? Jackie, Russell is a nice guy, but he's too old for you."

Jackie flung the door open and ran out into the hall. "I'm telling Mama how you waste toothpaste. No wonder she has to buy a new tube every week. And you don't rinse with the glass like you're supposed to."

Sharon's laughter followed Jackie into her room. Condescending, that's what her sister was. She would not — absolutely *would not* — stand for her sister looking down on her for one second.

The next morning, Jackie skipped out to the kitchen with a plan fully blossomed in her mind.

Unfortunately, the plan relied heavily on her mother's cooperation. Mrs. Howard listened with mounting skepticism as Jackie told her about the new guy she had met at Old Virginia City and how she wanted to invite him on a picnic in their woods.

When Jackie finished, Mrs. Howard hurled her usual road-blocks. "How old is this boy? Do you know his family? What do his parents do?"

"I didn't ask for his FBI file, Mama. How would I know all that? He's — he's good with animals and little children. You'd like him if you'd just give him a chance!" Don't lose your cool, she cautioned herself. If her mother had an inkling how much this meant to her, she'd never agree to a picnic in a million years.

"A picnic in the woods," Mrs. Howard said doubtfully. "Alone with a boy Sharon's age. . . ."

Jackie tried another angle. "Russell's interested in nature. Our woods have a creek with all sorts of neat things to look at. Moss and butterflies and stuff."

Her mother snorted. "Boys that age are hardly interested in butterflies. Don't be so naive."

"Who wouldn't be naive?" The last of her self-control shredded as she yelled, "Sharon says you're holding me back, and she's right! I can't do anything around here!"

Her mother stared at her. "I expect tantrums from your sister, but not from you."

"Sharon gets what she wants this way. Why shouldn't I?" Jackie didn't really want to be like her sister. All she wanted was to go on a picnic with Russell Bass. If screaming and yelling didn't work, she'd lie down in the middle of Lee Highway. "Mama, let me do something I want just this once."

Mrs. Howard sighed. "You're getting more like Sharon every day. You can have the picnic under one condition: Sharon has to go with you. You are much too young to be alone with a boy."

"*Shar-on!*" Jackie wailed. Having Sharon along on her romantic picnic with Russell was like inviting Dracula to a blood bank. But her mother remained firm. No Sharon, no picnic.

Maybe it was just as well. Russell could see them both together, and he'd have to choose. Of course, he'd pick the sister who loved him the most.

The picnic was arranged for Monday, Russell's day off from Old Virginia City. Sharon didn't have to go to work until after supper, so she was available.

Boy, was she ever available, Jackie thought, shaking paprika over a plate of deviled eggs. She'd been up since daybreak preparing the picnic basket — she wanted to be able to tell Russell she had fixed every crumb with her own two hands — while Sharon primped. The way to a man's heart was through his stomach, another of Mrs. Howard's corny sayings. Unwilling to leave anything to chance, Jackie packed thick ham and cheese sandwiches, deviled eggs, potato chips, pork and beans, homemade brownies, and oranges.

71

But Sharon evidently subscribed to the theory that the way to a man's heart was to blind him. She whirled into the kitchen wearing a cotton sundress and strippy-strappy sandals. Her glossy hair was drawn up into a high, ribbon-tied ponytail with a dewy pink rosebud tucked into the bow.

"What, no parasol?" Jackie licked mayonnaise off her fingertips.

Sharon nibbled a brownie crumb. "Haven't you ever seen the movie *Picnic*? Well, this is my Kim Novak look."

"I thought it was your Bertha Butt look."

"Picnics are supposed to be fun. You look like you're ready for a hike in the Sierras."

Jackie considered warning her sister of such mid-summer perils as snakes, poison ivy, spiders, blackberry thorns, and other deep woods dangers. Jackie's shoes might not be pretty, but she wouldn't sprain her ankle, either.

"He's here," said Mrs. Howard.

Russell Bass strode into the living room, greeted Mrs. Howard with a politeness that bordered on southern charm, then, hefting the picnic basket, escorted the girls across the yard. Because Jackie knew the path, now nearly obscured by the dense undergrowth, she led the way into the woods.

Within two minutes, she was sweating like a moose. Despite the leafy canopy that screened the burning sun, it was stuffy and close in the woods. Behind her, Sharon and Russell laughed over some joke. Jackie stopped to let them catch up. Russell helped Sharon over a rotted log.

With the picnic basket crooked over his elbow, he held an overhanging dogwood limb with one hand and assisted Sharon with the other.

Some romantic picnic this was turning out to be! Sharon was getting the Sir Walter Raleigh treatment while Jackie the Trailblazer was getting smacked by blackberry vines. As soon as they reached the creek, though, all that would change. Anxious to impress Russell on her own turf and get Sharon away from mean old rotten logs, Jackie plunged through the underbrush with renewed purpose, hurdling the Civil War rail fence like a white-tailed deer.

She could hear the creek before she actually saw it. Water burbled crisply over stones, sounding like a much larger stream than it was. She walked stilt-legged down the steep hill, then ran the rest of the way. Behind her, Sharon and Russell scrambled down the embankment, shrieking with laughter.

"Well," Jackie said simply. "Here we are."

She hoped Russell wouldn't be too disappointed. She loved this place, but it might not look like much to anyone else. Only a few feet wide, the creek flowed through a network of twigs and leaves snagged on drowned branches. The sun arrowed through a break in the trees. Waterbugs, their whiplike legs dimpling the surface, skittered along like miniature seaplanes. The waterbugs' pinpoint feet made shadows as big and round as pennies and the striped minnows that darted around the rocks were doubled against the muddy creekbed.

"Hey, this is great," Russell said enthusiastically. "You're lucky to have such a nice place on your own property."

Jackie smiled in relief. "Glad you like it. Well, let's eat."

"Not yet," Sharon said, in a new trilling voice, reminiscent of a bird somewhere in the woods calling the same three notes over and over. "Let's enjoy the grandeur of the woods."

Jackie nearly threw up. Grandeur of the woods! What was with Sharon all of a sudden? Did she really think she could compete with Jackie in Jackie's very own special place?

"Okay, we'll take a walk," she said agreeably.

Jackie led the way again, purposely tackling the difficult bends of the mossy-banked creek. Maybe her sister would slip and fall in. Pushing aside willow streamers that dipped into the water, Jackie said, "Hey, Russell, look at this." She pointed out a sandbar spangled with pawprints. "Raccoon tracks. They come down here to wash their food. They're very clean animals."

"Jackie knows all about animals," Sharon bragged, generous as she was gorgeous. "She has all these books. I bet she knows every bird there is." She favored Russell with a look that was at once demure and sizzling.

Russell stumbled over a root, apparently trapped in Sharon's sticky web. "It's good to know about things," he said. What happened to him? Jackie wondered. At the pony ride, he seemed capable of carrying on an intelligent conversa-

74

tion, but in Sharon's presence he was reduced to such absurdities as "it's good to know about things."

Well, she'd show him. She didn't just know about trees and birds — she knew lots of stuff.

"I can spell the longest word in the dictionary," she proclaimed. She had taught herself this years before, thinking it might come in handy one day.

Russell grinned. "Really? What *is* the longest word?"

"Antidisestablishmentarianism," Jackie replied, stumbling only a few times on the pronounciation. "Want to hear? Okay, here goes." She took a deep breath and began. "A-n-t-i-d-i-s-e-s-t-a-b-l-i-s-h — "

Sharon started laughing. "Jackie! You don't have to spell the whole thing."

Jackie frowned at her. Darn Sharon for wrecking her concentration. "Who ever heard of spelling half a word?"

"You don't even know what it means," her sister said.

"I do, too."

"What, then?"

"It's . . . uh . . ." When she memorized the spelling, she'd barely looked at the definition. "Something about a church being torn down," she faltered. Who cared what it meant anyway? A word with that many letters ought to be impressive just by itself.

Sharon and Russell cracked up.

"I'm glad you find me so amusing," Jackie said

coldly. A couple of hyenas, that's what they were.

"We're not laughing at you," Russell reassured her. "What you said was so funny."

"Are you guys ready to eat now?" She'd better hurry and win Russell's heart through his stomach before the eggs spoiled or something.

"Oh, let's wait a bit," Sharon said. Jackie fumed. This was *her* picnic, not Sharon's.

Russell asked Jackie, "Is that a little island? Can we get to it from here?"

"Sure," Jackie replied. "Just wade over. The water's only a few inches deep. Except where there are holes." How she'd love to see her sister swallowed up in a big sink hole.

"There's a log that goes almost all the way over," Russell said. "Sharon? Want to try it?"

"Of course. It looks beautiful over there." Sharon held out her hand. Suddenly she seemed unable to walk a step without Russell's assistance.

"Did you leave your cane at home?" Jackie asked sarcastically, but Sharon merely simpered as her dainty sandalled feet got sprinkled with a droplet of water. Russell, who was already across the log, leaned over, grasped Sharon around the waist, and swung her onto the mossy island.

It was a very tiny island. There wasn't room for Jackie. Determined to astound Russell with her knowledge of nature, Jackie left them alone and roved the creekbank for unusual plants.

Russell was supposed to fall madly in love with *her* in this romantic setting. Instead he seemed more interested in her sister, which wasn't fair, because Sharon already had a boy- friend. A minor detail Sharon probably neglected to mention to Russell.

A rugged outdoorsy guy like Russell couldn't help but admire a girl who knew about the woods. Jackie gathered samples of toothwort and Mayapple and skunk cabbage, then added yellow violets to her bouquet before heading back to the island.

She stopped abruptly, guarded from view by a veil of willow boughs.

Russell and Sharon were kissing. Not a sprightly little isn't-this-a-pretty-day peck but a real kiss. A long *long* kiss, too long to qualify for casual friendship.

Jackie was stunned. *Her* boyfriend, *her* creek. Sharon had stolen them both in one swoop. The skunk cabbage fell from her hand. Turning away from the disgusting spectacle, she tossed a stick into the water. It fought against the current for a second, then gave in, swirling downstream. Jackie watched the stick vanish around a bend, experiencing the same lonely feeling as when one of her favorite programs was over, only this was worse.

Much, much worse.

Chapter 8

Jackie wanted to run back up the hill over the Civil War fence, tear through briars and brambles, never halting until she was in her own room with the door shut. Leave the lovebirds to hunt their own way back. But it was still her picnic, even if Sharon had ruined it.

No, she'd wait a decent interval for Russell and Sharon to finish kissing, then she'd cheerfully announce it was time to eat. Too bad she didn't have a gong. How long was a decent interval? What if they started another kiss and went on like that the whole afternoon? She could starve for all they cared.

"Lunch time!" Jackie called, loud enough to discourage any more smooching. "Are you guys ready now?"

From the sheepish looks on their faces, Russell

and Sharon were definitely not ready. They left the island, holding hands.

"I'm famished," Russell declared, rather too heartily. "Bring on the grub, Cupcake." He put his arm around Jackie's shoulder, affectionately, like a big brother.

Jackie twisted away from him. Five minutes ago she would have swooned with joy to have Russell touch her. "I tried to get you to eat earlier, but you had *other* ideas," she said knowingly.

Her sister and Russell exchanged a loaded glance. Let them worry, Jackie thought. If they weren't supposed to be kissing, then they should have controlled themselves.

Because the ground beside the creek was too damp, Jackie selected a pair of logs as a picnic site. Russell and Sharon cozied up on the shortest log, sitting so close a piece of tissue paper shot from a bazooka couldn't have been wedged between them. Jackie sat by herself on the other log and glared at her sister. Whatever happened to "One for all and all for one?" The way this picnic had gone, it was obviously all for Sharon.

Russell ate three sandwiches and five deviled eggs, plus enormous helpings of everything else. He lavished compliments on Jackie, undoubtedly trying to make up for paying so much attention to Sharon.

"These eggs are the best I've ever had," he said. "What's the secret ingredient?"

Love, she nearly confessed. But she replied curtly, "Pickle juice."

"Are you a good cook?" Russell asked Sharon.

Sharon had scarcely eaten two bites. "I'm terrible. I can't even boil water."

Since Sharon was being so honest, Jackie decided to take advantage of the opening and discredit her sister a little further. "You should have seen the awful birthday cake Sharon baked for my birthday. The icing wouldn't stay on."

"It was a mess," Sharon admitted, laughing.

"And she's afraid to crack an egg," Jackie went on. "She made Mama break the eggs for my cake." Just so Russell would know he could forget any more delicious deviled eggs if he chose Sharon over her.

"Eggs are so icky," said Sharon with a mock shudder.

"She even burns spaghetti sauce." But Jackie could see she was losing points instead of gaining them. Russell wasn't interested in her sister's ability to crack eggs. Sharon's other talents more than made up for her mishaps in the kitchen.

Russell and Sharon chatted about school — Russell was going to George Mason University in the fall — while Jackie cleaned up the picnic litter. On the way back, Jackie once again blazed the trail, a good sport to the very last. Russell and Sharon lagged behind, taking forever to climb the hill.

Jackie walked with Sharon to Russell's car, determined to let them see she didn't care. Russell ruffled her hair, the way he rumpled the pony's mane.

"I had a great time," he said. "Best picnic I've

been on in my life. You coming to the park to-morrow, Jackie?"

What did he care? Unless . . . was it possible he still liked her? "I might," said Jackie, lifting her chin. "But I'll probably be busy."

"I hope you can," Russell said. "You really brighten the place up." To Sharon he added in a meaningful tone, "I'll see you tomorrow."

"See you." Sharon's own voice was low and throaty.

A simple farewell, yet brimming with emotion. Sharon waved at Russell's retreating car as if he were off to Antarctica. Jackie watched, too, her heart breaking.

On long summer evenings, Jackie and Sharon used to take an old quilt outside to a certain spot in the backyard, near the purple martin house Jackie had begged her father to build to her spec-ifications, and which no self-respecting bird had ever set claw in. Here, the ground rose slightly and the grass was silky and soft.

They'd spread the quilt like a beach blanket and lie down. Sharon's cat Felix would join them, reveling in the luxury of a blanket in the middle of the yard, switching his tail at the ro-bins blip-blipping across the lawn in search of worms.

"Is that a bat?" Sharon would ask when a bird scalloped across the mint-green sky. "No, it's a swallow," Jackie would reply. A little later she'd say, "There goes a bat," pointing to a flittery creature diving for insects on the wing. Sharon never could tell the difference between a swallow and a bat.

Cocooned in the hushed twilight, they would talk about dreams they'd had or their wishes for the future. Jackie always had the worst dreams, in lurid color, about savage dogs or plane crashes, but Sharon had the most fantastic aspirations.

"I'm going to Hollywood," she'd murmur, "and be a famous movie actress, like Elizabeth Taylor. People tell me I look like her when she was young. What are you going to be?"

By comparison, Jackie's ambitions were homely and meager, like the booklets she made in school with the crayoned titles sliding downhill because she forgot to use a ruler. "I'd like to be the person who names the new schools," she'd say. "I'd use all flower names for the grade schools and tree names for the junior highs. You know, like Dogwood Junior High."

Sharon thought this was funny. "How about Bachelor Button Elementary?" she'd splutter. And Jackie would laugh, too, because it did sound funny, under the endless expanse of dusky sky.

This summer Sharon didn't get home from her job until quarter to ten, too late to lie outside with dew falling. Not that Jackie wanted to share a blanket or even the same hemisphere with her Benedict Arnold sister.

The evening after the disastrous picnic, Jackie couldn't bear to be in the next room to that traitor, her sister. She lugged the musty old quilt from the bottom of the linen closet and went outdoors. The purple martin house, with its compartments on all four sides and peaked roof, looked like a haunted house for birds. The white paint had worn to a grubby gray and the pole tilted like the Leaning Tower of Pisa. Mr. Howard wanted to take the disgraceful thing down, but Jackie wouldn't let him, always hopeful that a purple martin family might move in. Now it seemed unlikely that the birdhouse would ever be inhabited.

Sharon came out, dressed for work. "What are you doing out here all by yourself?"

"Trying to be alone." Jackie did not look at her; instead she pictured the birdhouse rammed over her sister's head.

Sharon sat down on the quilt, folding her legs beneath her so she wouldn't muss her skirt. "You haven't said five words since we came back from the picnic yesterday."

"What's there to say?"

"Russell had a nice time. So did I. A picnic by the creek was a really good idea."

"I could see you two were having a ball." Jackie plucked a blade of grass and tore it into a dozen pieces. "Why did you do it?" she asked suddenly, unable to keep the anguish out of her voice.

"Do what?"

"Take him away from me. I told you I liked him, and you deliberately stole him." Tears welled in her eyes but she blinked them back valiantly. She'd never ever cry in front of her sister again.

"Jackie." Sharon's voice was soothing, like the

time Jackie left her lucky rabbit's foot in the dentist's office. "Russell Bass is practically nineteen. He's much too old for you."

"He's too old for you, too!" Jackie sobbed in spite of herself. "You're only sixteen."

"Almost seventeen. I didn't plan what happened at the picnic. Russell's been coming to my booth the last few days to talk and when we were alone on the island — well, things just sort of clicked."

"Yeah, like lips." Jackie wished she could stop crying.

"Hey, Russell likes you a lot. He thinks you're cute and . . . what was the word he used? Refreshing."

"Did he — did he say that?" Jackie snuffled.

Sharon nodded. "He also said you can fix him a picnic any day of the week."

"Really?" Maybe she still had a chance! It was entirely possible that Russell would get tired of Sharon's boring old beauty and come back to Jackie, who was refreshingly cute.

Sharon shook her hair in the breeze. "I forgot how nice it was out here. When you work like I do, you don't have time to enjoy birds and trees very much." She made it sound as though she punched a time clock in a salt mine.

"You don't *have* to work," Jackie said. Maybe Sharon would realize how fast the summer was passing and quit her job.

"I know. But I want to. Remember when we used to come out here and talk about what we'd do and stuff?" Her sister was definitely in a reflective mood.

"I remember you used to make fun of what I said I wanted to be."

"Oh, that business about naming the schools. It was funny."

"No funnier than wanting to be a movie actress," Jackie countered. Their mother once told them never to trample someone else's dreams, no matter how slight, but of course that advice went in one ear and out the other where Sharon was concerned.

Sharon stood up. "Well, I've got to leave. You coming with Dad later to pick me up?"

Jackie nearly said no. If she never saw Old Virginia City again, it would be too soon. But that would be surrendering to her sister, letting Sharon have Russell. He thought Jackie was cute, and he liked the way she cooked. Maybe he'd only kissed Sharon to be polite, though she sincerely doubted it. One thing was crystal clear, she'd never win if she never went back.

"Tell Russell I'll be there," Jackie said, planning to be especially cute and refreshing. Maybe Russell would reconsider and choose the *right* sister.

Mr. Howard fooled around in the garden until nearly nine-thirty. By the time they pulled into the parking lot, Sharon was waiting outside the gate. Jackie didn't even have time to get out of the car, much less sprint down the concourse and act cute and refreshing around Russell.

"Move over," Sharon said, squeezing into the front seat with Jackie.

Jackie instantly spied the class ring sparkling

on Sharon's left hand, bound up with a strip of napkin to keep it from slipping off her finger. The red stone gleamed in the parking lot lights.

"Whose is that?" Jackie demanded. Mick Rowe's class ring had a blue stone. Sharon wore it on a chain when she wasn't wearing the mustard-seed necklace he had given her for her birthday. Tonight, though, both the necklace and Mick's ring were conspicuously absent.

"It's Russell's," Sharon whispered. "He gave it to me when he asked me to go with him."

Jackie suppressed the urge to push her sister through the windshield. Sharon was going steady with the boy *she* loved! She didn't even have a chance to win him back. But she couldn't let Sharon know how devastated she was, wouldn't give her sister the *satisfaction*. She'd pretended it meant nothing to her. Less than nothing, even.

Jackie's resolve lasted almost twenty-four hours before it unraveled completely.

The next evening Sharon came to dinner flaunting Russell Bass's class ring on her finger, now more permanently strapped with adhesive tape, and Mick Rowe's mustard-seed necklace clasped around her throat.

"Mama," Jackie complained, "Sharon's going steady with two boys at the same time. Isn't that illegal?"

Her mother passed a platter of fried squash. Tonight they were having an all-vegetable dinner, fresh-picked from the garden. "I don't know how legal it is, but it certainly doesn't make much sense. Sharon, why *are* you going with two boys at once? Can't you make up your mind?"

Sharon grabbed the first ear of corn from the bowl. "Well, no," she replied, somewhat embarrassed. "But I don't want to lose either one, so I'm going with both. For a while, at least."

"Traitor," Jackie said under her breath.

"What did you say?" Sharon said.

"I said traitor! Benedict Arnold. Poor Mick, up there in the mountains, thinking you're being faithful to him at home. How would you like it if he did that to you?"

Sharon speared a slice of tomato. "He might be, for all I know. Mick and I didn't make any promises to each other this summer. I kept his ring because it was easier than going through the folderol of breaking up."

Jackie refused to let it go. "I think it's crummy, after he bought you that necklace and everything. A class ring is forever. Isn't that right, Daddy?"

"Sharon's love life is her business," Mr. Howard answered levelly. Jackie should have known better than to try to involve her father. He made every effort to avoid getting embroiled in the girls' squabbles, especially during mealtime.

"But the mustard seed symbolizes faithfulness!" Jackie cried. "Only a . . . a hypocrite would wear a mustard seed necklace from one boy and a class ring from another!"

"Are you calling me a hypocrite?" Sharon buttered a second ear of corn. The way Sharon ate corn reminded Jackie of a cartoon character, gnawing the cob from one end to the other like a typewriter carriage. She half-expected to hear a little "ding" when Sharon got to the end of a row.

"And another thing," Jackie said. "How come she's eating vegetables from the garden? Sharon quit the garden, remember, Mama? She said she hated the stuff we grew and since she didn't eat it, she didn't have to do the work."

"I do seem to recall some remark about how common it was to hoe corn," Mrs. Howard said mildly.

Sharon sprang up from the table, her face red. "I suppose going with two boys at once is common, too! All anybody ever does around here is criticize me! I'm glad I only have a year left of high school. I can't wait to leave this place!"

"Sharon — " Mrs. Howard began. "Nobody said a word about your going with two boys. You said that yourself."

"Jackie did!"

"She was just teasing. We all were." Mrs. Howard patted Sharon's chair. "Now sit down and eat your supper."

Sharon stomped over to the trash can and dramatically scraped her entire plate into the bin. "The next time you have a vegetable dinner please be kind enough to inform me. I'll fix myself a peanut butter and jelly sandwich. I wouldn't dare touch one morsel I'm not entitled to."

"Sharon, you're being silly. Sit down. I'll get you another plate," Mrs. Howard coaxed. "Sweet corn's your favorite."

"Not any more. Anyway, I'm not hungry,"

Sharon declared airily. "I'm in love. People in love don't have any appetite."

"You can't live on love," said Mr. Howard.

"*I* can," Sharon replied, defiant as ever. With that, she flounced out of the room.

Mr. Howard sighed. "Another wonderful meal. Do you want to go talk to her or should I?"

"I will, in a minute." Mrs. Howard glanced sharply at Jackie. "It's partly your fault. You started the argument."

Jackie wasn't the tiniest bit sorry she had caused Sharon to leave the table. Traitors didn't deserve to eat good fresh corn and squash. Let Sharon eat her stale old pretzels at work. Let her live on love, see where *that* gets her.

Chapter 9

"Here. I don't need these anymore." Jackie dumped an armload of objects on her sister's messy bed.

Sharon had only cleaned her room two or three times in her life. Mrs. Howard was always threatening to report her to the Board of Health. Now that she was working and had even less time to not clean, Sharon's room looked like the site of a rumble.

"What *is* all this stuff?" Sharon picked up an ugly stretched-out sweater with a purple stain on one sleeve. "This used to be mine. I gave it to you a long time ago."

"And I'm giving it back," Jackie stated. "Plus all the other things that used to be yours. I don't want them any more."

Sharon sifted through the pile. Two sweaters. A pair of pants. Three tops. A belt made out of chewing gum wrappers, intricately braided and shellacked, that Sharon had made in Brownies. Six Nancy Drew books. And a tiny bottle with a shiny new penny inside.

"I got this in Williamsburg, on a field trip," Sharon said, rattling the penny in its bottle. "You kept bugging me for it until I let you have it."

"Well, you can have it back." Jackie pulled a sheet of notebook paper from her pocket. "This is an inventory of all the stuff you've given me over the years. I believe you'll find everything here." She presented the list to her sister with a military gesture. "Sign the bottom. That's my receipt."

Sharon skimmed the paper, then looked up at Jackie. "Why are you doing this?"

"I don't want anything that belongs to a traitor," Jackie replied haughtily.

"Traitor?" Sharon repeated, as if she had no idea what Jackie was talking about.

"Don't you understand plain English?" Jackie shouted. "Traitor! Backstabber! Two-face! Boyfriend-nabber!"

Sharon folded the ugly green sweater as if it were made of the finest cashmere. "Ahhh. Now I understand. You're still sore because Russell asked me to go with him."

"Sore isn't the word for it. You deliberately stole him from me, Sharon Howard! And you already have a boyfriend. You don't need two!" Jackie was so angry, she could feel the ligaments in her neck standing out like cords.

"Jackie, I don't know how many times I have to say this: I did not steal Russell from anyone, much less my own sister." When Jackie opened her mouth to protest, Sharon asked, "Were you going with Russell Bass?"

"No, but — "

"Did he ever ask you out?"

"He never had time — you moved in on him as soon as you saw him." Jackie inhaled deeply. "I'm going to get him back."

"Oh, really? How?"

Jackie wasn't sure how. Maybe she could take a picture of Sharon wearing that disgusting sweater and those awful pants with the hole in the knee — Sharon's old hand-me-downs that were good enough for Jackie once. She'd show the picture to Russell. After one look, he'd demand his ring back. If only it were that easy.

"I know," she said, suddenly inspired. "I'll tell Russell the truth about you. He'd break it off in a jiffy if he knew what you were *really* like."

"What truth?" Sharon said, actually looking concerned.

"Like how you always open your Christmas presents as soon as you find them, instead of waiting for Christmas day. And the time you jammed your history book in a phone booth and claimed it was lost and then some kid turned it in and Mama had to pay for it." She could have plumbed that bottomless source of material all day, but Sharon interrupted with a relieved giggle.

"As long as you're slinging mud," Sharon said, "I could tell Russell how you never brushed your teeth. You just wet your toothbrush when Mom came in to check."

"I did not!"

"Or what about the time you threw up at the parade? That ought to turn him off quick. Boys aren't too crazy over girls who get sick in public."

"I couldn't help it," Jackie said defensively. "Daddy made me laugh. He said Santa Claus probably went ho, ho, ho all night because he kept saying it all the way down Prescott Avenue. I couldn't stop laughing and then I got sick, but that was because I really had the whooping cough, only we didn't know it yet."

But she saw Sharon's point. A smear campaign against her sister would only backfire. For every bad thing Jackie dredged up about Sharon, Sharon could retaliate with five bad things about Jackie. That was the problem with being born last — Sharon had a longer memory and a bigger arsenal supply.

"Sign the paper," Jackie ordered.

"For heaven's sake, Jackie. We're not going to court over a bunch of old clothes!"

"I don't trust traitors. My receipt, please."

Sharon placed the list on top of the pile. "Okay, since you're being so stubborn . . . there's something missing."

"What?"

"Ellsworth."

Sharon had brought the stuffed elephant back from a visit to her grandmother's in Bristol years before. Like most of Sharon's possessions, Ellsworth wound up forgotten under Sharon's bed until Jackie rescued the stuffed animal one day while Sharon was at school. Jackie dressed the elephant in an old blouse which she thought

93

made a beautiful christening gown. Sharon let Jackie have Ellsworth "on loan," like a library book. Jackie loved the stuffed animal more than any doll. Even more than her sister, sometimes.

It was low of Sharon to bring up Ellsworth. Very low indeed. But what else could you expect from a traitor?

"I don't know where Ellsworth is," Jackie fibbed. She knew exactly where the elephant was, in a box on her closet shelf.

"I'm not signing anything till you find Ellsworth." Sharon gave the list back to Jackie. "Then we'll be even."

"We'll never be even," Jackie said bitterly. "Not as long as you still have my boyfriend!"

"Are you and Sharon fighting again?" Mrs. Howard asked Jackie after Sharon had gone to work.

Bored and lonely, Jackie fidgeted in her parents' room while her mother hemmed a sundress Sharon had recently bought. For lack of anything better to do, she pawed through her mother's jewelry case. "Is that what Sharon says?"

"No, but it looks to me like you two are fighting. It's about that boy, isn't it?"

"What boy?" Jackie looped a strand of beads over her ears and across her forehead, thinking she looked exotic. But her image in the mirror didn't look exotic at all, just a dumb kid with notched bangs and a necklace on her head.

"You know what boy. Russell Bass." Her mother bit off a thread because Jackie was using the scissors to trim a piece of hair.

"You're not supposed to do that," Jackie said. "It's bad for your teeth."

"Then stop taking my scissors." Mrs. Howard snipped the thread properly. "And don't get off the subject. We were talking about Sharon and Russell."

"What's to talk about?" Jackie rummaged in the top tray of her mother's jewelry case, tangling necklaces and bracelets. "Sharon is going with Russell Bass. She's also going with Mick Rowe. It's a free country. She can go with a hundred boys if she wants."

"I don't think Sharon's too happy with the arrangement," Mrs. Howard said.

"She doesn't act like she's losing any sleep over it." Jackie selected a pin shaped like a turtle and clipped it to her T-shirt. "Can I borrow this some time?"

"Yes. Quit digging in my jewlery. You've got everything in a jumble. I know you had a crush on Russell Bass, but that boy is simply too old for you, Jackie."

How could her mother make her feelings for Russell sound so demeaning? A crush. Jackie didn't have a crush. She was *in love*. There was a vast difference. But because she wasn't sixteen like her sister, nobody took her seriously.

"It doesn't matter whether he's too old or not," Jackie said flatly. "He's going with Sharon."

Mrs. Howard rethreaded her needle. "I was wrong about Sharon working. That job has really been good for her. She doesn't bug me about the car like she used to."

Sharon's job *had* changed things in the Howard house. Aside from the obvious change in the evening routine, there was another subtle, almost imperceptible difference that Jackie couldn't quite put her finger on.

She was reminded of the time she tried to teach herself chess. The game was too hard, but she enjoyed setting the plastic figures in the proper order on the board. Sharon would sneak into Jackie's room and switch the white queen with the black king or balance a pawn on top of the castle. Some little thing. Jackie never caught her sister but she knew Sharon was the culprit. And Sharon was still doing it, making niggling changes. This whole summer, Jackie thought, was like a pawn out of place on a chess board.

"If only she wasn't so flighty about boys," Mrs. Howard commented, still talking about Sharon.

Jackie took the onyx necklace and earrings out of the chest. Today, she derived no comfort in finding the jewelry in its usual place.

"Can I have the black stone set when I'm older?" Jackie asked her mother.

"I've already promised it to Sharon." Naturally! "She wants to wear it on her wedding day as something borrowed."

"What am I supposed to wear on my wedding day?" Jackie demanded sullenly. "Ellsworth? She's borrowed. I borrowed her from Sharon about a thousand years ago." She imagined the stuffed elephant perched on top of her veil.

Her mother laughed. "I'm going to let you

have the Australian diamond." When he was in the Navy, Mr. Howard won a diamond engagement ring a jilted sailor had raffled.

Jackie loved the Australian diamond, but she wanted first choice. As usual, Sharon beat her to it. Sharon would always be first. In the middle tray along with the miniature horseshoe, she found Sharon's fifth-grade school picture.

"How come you keep this in here with your good stuff?"

"I don't know," her mother replied, glancing at the snapshot. "I never thought about it."

"All our other school pictures are in the album," Jackie persisted. "You don't have one of me in here. Just Sharon."

Her mother put down her sewing. "Jackie, what are you driving at? Are you jealous because I have an old picture of Sharon in my jewelry box?"

"No, I'm not jealous. If you want to keep a picture of Sharon and not one of me I don't care! I couldn't care less!" Tossing the rest of her mother's jewelry back in the case, Jackie slammed the chest on the dresser. "And you can let Sharon have the Australian diamond, too. I'm never going to get married, and I wouldn't want it to go to waste."

"Jackie, what is wrong with you this evening?" Her mother felt Jackie's forehead. "You don't have a temperature."

Jackie smoothed her bangs down again. "I'm not sick."

Her mother smiled. "I guess we're all a little

cranky from the heat. How would you like to go with Sharon tomorrow night? Have a little fun at Old Virginia City. Okay?"

She'd see Russell again! But did she want to? After all, he was going with her two-faced sister. Jackie still loved him, even if he had picked Sharon over her. Like the papery moths that fluttered around the porch light every night, she couldn't keep away from Russell Bass.

Russell was currying Cookie when Jackie walked up. "Hey there, Cupcake. Where've you been lately? I've missed you."

"You have?" Jackie was astounded. "Even with Sharon around?"

He laughed. "Sharon is Sharon. You're you. Nobody can take your place, remember that."

That was the nicest thing anyone had ever told her. Suddenly shy, Jackie handed him a lunch bag. "I brought you a snack. I thought you might be tired of pretzels." Although he probably wasn't tired of the pretzel-seller.

He peeked into the sack. "A sandwich. And an orange. Aren't you a sweetie? Thanks."

"And two carrots for the ponies." Jackie climbed up on the fence. "Can I help you comb Cookie?" Lazy old Sharon would never offer to do that.

"Sorry. I'm the only one allowed to handle the animals. Something about insurance." He looked up at her, his blue eyes crinkled with concern. "Business is so slow, I'm afraid Mr. Powell's going to start letting people go."

"Not you!" Jackie cried. "The ponies won't

like it if you leave." Upset, she lost her balance and tumbled off the fence into the sawdust.

Russell rushed over and helped her to her feet. "Are you okay? That was quite a spill."

"I'm fine," Jackie said, wishing she could lie there forever. Maybe she should pretend her back was broken . . . Russell would scoop her up in his arms, exclaim she was lighter than a feather, and then —

"You better go see your sister," Russell advised. "If you're hurt, Mr. Powell will want to know."

She wasn't hurt, at least not physically, but she walked up to Sharon's booth. Only one customer was being served, a familiar-looking blond boy. It was Mick Rowe, Sharon's other boyfriend! What was *he* doing at Old Virginia City?

"Look who's here!" Sharon greeted Jackie with forced gaiety. "Mick's home early from camp, isn't that *wonderful*?"

"Hi, Mick. What a great tan."

"Hello, Jackie. You're pretty tanned yourself," Mick said.

"From slaving in the garden." Jackie noticed Russell's class ring lying behind the mustard dispenser. Mick's class ring bobbled from a chain around Sharon's neck. "How'd you find out where Sharon was?" she asked Mick.

He waited for Sharon to drizzle cheese on the hot doughy pretzel. "I called your house, and your mother told me she was working. I was coming by anyway, so I just popped in to surprise Sharon."

"Boy, was she *ever* surprised," Jackie said emphatically.

Sharon shot her a save-me look and nudged Russell's class ring toward her. Jackie palmed the ring before Mick reached for the mustard.

"Mick," said Sharon. "How was camp?"

Mick described the rigors of a counselor's life. Sharon appeared to be listening intently, but Jackie knew her sister was borderline frantic. Then she saw Sharon's eyes widen at something behind her. Jackie turned.

Russell was heading their way!

Sharon reacted swiftly. "Here comes the owner! I can't let him see me goofing off. You'll have to leave, Mick."

"Okay," Mick said amiably. "Maybe we can go to the movies tomorrow."

As soon as Mick left, Sharon dropped Mick's class ring down the neck of her shirt. "Give me Russell's ring!"

Disgusted, Jackie handed the ring to her sister, who slipped it back on her finger as if it had never been off. Boys as nice as Mick and Russell didn't deserve such deceitful treatment.

"Cover for me?" her sister pleaded.

"Why should I?"

"Because," Sharon said. "You're my sister."

And Sharon *was* her sister, but that hadn't stopped her from stealing Jackie's boyfriend. Sharon always reminded Jackie of family ties when it suited her purpose. Suddenly Jackie wanted to be the one to switch the playing pieces on the chess board, change the order just a bit.

100

Chapter 10

With Mick back in town, Sharon began leading a double life.

On Tuesday she went to an afternoon movie with Mick and out to McDonald's for a before-work-hamburger with Russell. Jackie stayed home and dusted her china cat collection. On Wednesday Sharon went swimming with Russell, then to an early evening concert with Mick. Jackie alphabetized the nature guides in her bookcase, tempted to leave *Reptiles and their Kin* in Sharon's room. On Thursday Sharon and Mick went to a cook-out while Jackie helped her mother in the garden.

Jackie wouldn't even have known about these dates except that Sharon checked with her to make sure she wasn't wearing the same outfit twice in a row and the fact that Jackie stationed herself near the door in order to see what was going on. She was disgusted at the way her sister managed to dangle both boys.

Sharon came into Jackie's room. Today, Friday, Russell was scheduled to pick her up for a quick lunch before a special meeting at Old Virginia City. "Does this look all right?" she asked Jackie. "I can't remember if I wore this skirt Monday or Wednesday. I don't think Russell's seen me in it since Tuesday night."

Jackie barely spared her sister a glance. All morning she'd futilely dialed WPGC, still trying to get through and win a free album. "So why don't you hire a secretary to keep track of your clothes along with your dates?"

"Do you think I like this?" Sharon hooked her hair behind one ear. "I certainly didn't plan on Mick coming back from camp early. But I already accepted Russell's ring so I couldn't very well give it back to him and say, 'Sorry, but my real boyfriend is in town now.' "

"That would be the honest thing to do, but of course, you wouldn't know about honesty."

"Well, it isn't easy, juggling Russell and Mick so they don't find out about each other."

Jackie rubbed her thumb and index finger together. "See this? It's the world's smallest violin playing 'My Heart Bleeds for You.' "

"For heaven's sake, will you get off it?" Sharon brushed her hair so it flipped up, then rebrushed it so the ends turned under again.

"I wish you wouldn't use my brush," Jackie said. "If I use yours you scream cooties. Now I'll have to boil it."

"My hair is clean. I just washed it." Sharon washed her hair before each date, even if she had two the same day. Jackie was hoping her sister's hair would fall out from so much washing. No such luck. Sharon's hair was as bouncy and shiny as ever.

Felix ambled into Jackie's room. Lately the cat had taken to napping on Jackie's bed.

Jackie petted him. "Felix is my old buddy now, aren't you? He likes me best. You might not have a cat when you come home tonight," she added to her sister.

"I might not have a job when I come home tonight," Sharon said dolefully.

"Why?" Maybe the owner of Old Virginia City found out his pretzel-seller was two-timing the pony-ride leader. The man had a reputation to maintain; the park *was* a family place.

"This meeting we're having. Russell thinks Mr. Powell is getting us together for some lay-offs. Business has been terrible."

"I'm not surprised. It's a stupid park. After you've been once, who'd ever want to go back?" Jackie wished she'd never heard of Old Virginia City. If they hadn't gone that first night, Sharon wouldn't have gotten the job, and Jackie wouldn't have met Russell, and Sharon wouldn't have stolen him from Jackie.

"It's okay for little kids. But attendance has been way down the last few weeks. If things don't improve, Mr. Powell will have to close down." A horn beeped outside. "There's Russell. Gotta run." Sharon planted a kiss between her cat's ears. "See you guys."

Jackie passed the long dull afternoon playing war with her mother, a game that made them both lethargic with its endless repetition. The only sounds were the ticking of the kitchen clock and the slap-slap of cards. Felix dozed on the cool linoleum under the table.

Some Sister Rebellion, Jackie thought. She and her mother both turned up sevens, but neither called out "War." She had joined forces with Sharon to fight for their independence and have a great summer. After Sharon got *her* job and *her* boyfriends, she conveniently forgot about the other half of the agreement.

Jackie heard Russell's car pull into the driveway around four. Scattering her cards, she ran outside. "Hi, Russell!" she chirped, leaning into the driver's window.

"Hey there, Cupcake." His smile was so warm, she nearly melted into a puddle. "What've you been up to?"

"Nothing much." She looked at Sharon, still sitting in the passenger seat. "Aren't you going to get out?"

"In a minute." Her sister pulled the rearview mirror toward her and checked her hair. "We have the most exciting news."

"You're engaged to Mr. Powell," Jackie quipped. Russell laughed appreciatively.

Sharon frowned. "No, silly. It's about the meeting. Things are so bad at the park, Mr. Powell's cutting back the hours the park will be open. We're opening at three instead of ten in the morning now."

"That's exciting news?" Jackie asked.

"Mr. Powell was going to let some people go, but Russell came up with this really nifty idea." Sharon nudged Russell. "You tell it. It's your idea."

Russell shook his head modestly. "You tell it. You're better at that than I am."

"Tell *what*?" Jackie said.

Sharon answered, "Russell suggested printing fliers with a coupon for a free pony ride. That ought to bring in a lot of business. Mr. Powell said he'd have the fliers made tonight so we could distribute them tomorrow. Everybody can keep their jobs another few weeks, to see how Russell's idea works. Isn't that great?" She linked her arm through Russell's with a proprietary smile. "If the park succeeds, it'll be because of Russell."

"It's only until Labor Day," Russell told Jackie. "Most of the employees have to go back to school."

"So it'll close anyway," Jackie said.

"I think Mr. Powell plans to keep it open on weekends until the weather gets cold. Then he'll probably sell it," Russell replied.

Jackie thought of something. "Maybe Mr. Powell will let you keep Cookie and Ginger."

"I doubt that," he laughed.

"Jackie," Sharon's voice held an edge of warning. "I hear Mom calling you."

"I didn't hear her." She wasn't born yesterday. Her sister was only trying to get rid of her so she and Russell could smooch.

Sharon snuggled up to Russell. "Now we need people to stuff fliers in mailboxes," she said to him, obviously excluding Jackie from the conversation.

"There's you and me," Russell said. "We can cover a lot of territory in my car before we go in to work." He glanced up at Jackie. "Hey Jackie! You'll help us, won't you?"

"She's busy," Sharon answered quickly.

"No, I'm not! I'm not doing anything the whole day! I'm a good mailbox-stuffer!" She was not about to let her sister cheat her out of an opportunity to spend the day with Russell.

"You're a doll." He smiled at her, making the crinkles around his blue eyes deeper. "Mr. Powell will pay five dollars."

"I don't care," Jackie said eagerly. "I don't need the money. I'll do it for nothing." She'd give up breathing for him, if he asked.

"That's more than my brother would do," Russell remarked. "William wants a dollar just to pass the salt."

Sharon said, "I didn't know you had a brother."

"Yeah. He's Jackie's age."

"My age?" Jackie echoed, interested. "Your brother's thirteen?"

"Almost," Russell qualified. "He'll be twelve on his next birthday."

Sharon clapped her hands. "That's perfect! You bring William to help stuff mailboxes, and I'll bring Jackie."

"You're not *bringing* me anywhere," Jackie said acidly. "I already volunteered." Her sister was treating her like a piece of luggage or something.

"William will come, won't he?" Sharon asked Russell.

"For five dollars he will."

"Good. With your brother and Jackie on one team and you and I on another, we'll cover more ground."

Russell nodded. "Okay. I'll bring William. Pick you two up around nine, okay?" He kissed Sharon lightly on the lips.

Jackie looked away with a pang. Then she brightened. Tomorrow Russell might be kissing *her*, out of gratitude. She'd work really hard. And she'd be nice to his brother, even if he was only eleven. Anything for Russell. William was probably a younger version of his fantastic older brother, so how bad could it be?

Jackie was not prone to making hasty judgments, but at one single glance she decided William Bass was without a doubt the biggest drip she had ever encountered in her entire life.

Russell arrived on time, anxious to get going. Sharon slid across the front seat, leaving Jackie to share the back seat with William, who never even bothered to look up from his *Fantastic Four* comic as she got in the car.

"Sharon, Jackie, this is my brother William," Russell said, backing out of the driveway. "William, I'd like you to meet Sharon and her sister Jackie."

"Hi, Billy." Sharon waggled her fingers in greeting.

107

"My name," William said, enunciating every syllable as if he were in a national spelling bee, "is *Will*iam. Not Billy or Bill or Will. Okay?"

Charm boy, Jackie thought, noting the thick glasses, the pudgy build. Nothing, absolutely *nothing*, about William remotely resembled his older brother. "So," Jackie said, remembering her vow to be nice. "What school do you go to?"

William lowered his comic to regard Jackie with utter disdain. "I'd expect that question from a grown-up. Adults always ask things like 'what grade are you in?' and 'do you like school?' But not another kid."

"I'm not another kid," Jackie retorted. "I'm thirteen. Two years older than you."

"Really?" William sized her up. "I would have guessed around ten."

"Ten! You need — " She started to say he needed glasses, but since he was already wearing glasses it would have been unkind to call attention to his sight problem. William's *other* problems, however, were a different matter. The only way she could keep her blood pressure down was to ignore him.

Russell stopped by Old Virginia City to pick up the fliers. He returned to the car with a stack about a foot high.

"Do we have to distribute all those?" Sharon squawked.

"As many as we can," Russell said, after locking the fliers in the trunk. "Otherwise, Mr. Powell will lose more money. Those fliers weren't cheap to print."

"Can I drive, Russell?" Sharon wheedled.

"Please. I haven't driven in so long I'm afraid I'll forget how."

Russell didn't get all red-faced and bulgy-eyed like their father did whenever Sharon asked to drive the car. He simply handed Sharon the keys and got in on the other side. "Do you know where Fairfax Estates is?" He consulted the map Mr. Powell had provided with the areas marked for each distribution team.

"Sure. That's near Lanier Junior High. Let's go!" Sharon popped the gear and sped down the highway toward Fairfax Estates. Russell didn't seem to mind Sharon's wild driving in the least, but Jackie was relieved when they finally arrived. Although he didn't say anything, William must have been a bit perturbed too — he was still on the same page of his comic.

At the entrance of the development, Russell divided the fliers into four bunches, then showed the map to William and Jackie. "Sharon and I will take the eastern half. You guys cover the streets to the parkland. Put a flier in every single mailbox. No skipping houses, understand?"

William snapped his bubblegum arrogantly. "We're not infants. When do we get the five bucks?"

"When the job is done," Russell replied.

As Jackie and William set off up the incline to the first group of houses, Jackie realized that many kids she knew from school lived here. What would they think if they saw her stuffing mailboxes with a geek like William? She could hear Angel Allen, the self-crowned Miss Popularity of seventh grade, "Is that Jackie Howard with that creep? Boy, she must be hard up."

William, she discovered very quickly, was not only a drip, but a drag. At every mailbox, he stopped and folded each flier precisely into thirds. Then he put the red flag up.

"What are you doing that for?" Jackie asked.

"So people will know there's something in the box." He cast Jackie a withering glance.

"The flag means there's mail to be picked *up*. If the mailman sees it, he might take the fliers out again."

"No, he won't. There aren't any stamps on them." William creased another paper, placed it in the mailbox, and raised the flag.

"You're taking too long! We'll be on this street all day! Just stuff it in and go on to the next one."

"I do things my way, you do things your way."

"All right. We'll split up. I'll take the cross streets." She was positively itching to get away from him. Why did she ever let herself be talked into stuffing mailboxes with an eleven-year-old troll?

She went up to the first house on her street, crammed a flier any old which way into the mailbox, slammed it shut again, then trudged on to the next house. The houses seemed to march on forever.

All this work for a lousy five dollars. And Russell wasn't even around to be impressed with her diligence. He was off with Sharon, probably having a great time while Jackie was stuck with his beastly brother.

Why *was* she doing this, anyhow? What did she care if the amusement park stayed open? In fact, she'd like to see it fail. If the park closed, smart-alecky Sharon would be out of a job. She wouldn't have all that extra cash to buy clothes. And she wouldn't see Russell every day at work.

Old Virginia City stood for everything Jackie wasn't or didn't have.

"I quit!" Jackie said out loud, just like her sister the day Sharon went on strike in the garden.

Spying a storm grate, Jackie looked around to make sure no one saw her, then tossed the bundle of fliers down the drain.

Chapter 11

Jackie sat cross-legged on the well-cap, under the shade of the maple. She'd spent the last hour in the garden and it felt good to rest. Mr. Howard was still working, ripping weeds and morning glories with the Rototiller.

Leaning down, Jackie pushed her finger into the soft pushed-up earth near her feet. Moles had excavated the side yard into a maze of ridges. Her father threatened to stomp the tunnels, but Jackie argued that nobody used the side yard and that moles had a right to live, too.

Across the road, Nate's Garage was doing a brisk business. Cars whooshed up and down Lee Highway. Everybody had something to do, except Jackie, who felt as dull as the bumblebee going *zizz-zizz* in her mother's mock orange bush.

Jackie closed her eyes. When I open my eyes,

she said to herself, the first car I'll see will be red.

Jackie opened her eyes. The first car she saw was not red but blue, and it was turning into her driveway. It was Russell!

She leaped up, stumbling over a mole hill. "Russell!" she cried, running over to his car before he switched the engine off.

"Hey there, Cupcake." He climbed out, placing his sunglasses in his shirt pocket. He was wearing his cowboy shirt unbuttoned over a spanking white T-shirt and jeans. Jackie loved the way his clean white T-shirt fit into the waistband of his jeans without a wrinkle. It was the little things about Russell, she realized, that would do her in.

"Sharon's not here. She took my mother to the store. Mama actually let her drive, can you believe it? They just left so they won't be back for a while. Do you want to wait?" she asked hopefully.

"I have a few minutes before I have to leave for work. Your dad waved as I came up the driveway. That's some garden he's got."

"Yeah. Every year he claims he won't put one in because it's so much trouble," Jackie said. "But when the seed catalogs come in January, he changes his mind. Mama says it gives him something to do. I wish I had something to do. Summer's almost over, and I haven't done anything. This year's been a real bummer."

"What did you used to do in the summer?" Russell buffed a scratch on the fender with the tail of his shirt.

113

"Dumb stuff, mostly."

"Like what?"

"Well, I used to catch fireflies and put them in a jar. I always let them go." What was the matter with her, blathering on about catching fireflies? She wanted to impress him, not scare him off. But he was so easy to talk to.

"Hey, I did that, too," Russell admitted.

"You did? And I — you're going to think this is really stupid — but I made these little houses down by the creek."

"For the animals, you mean?"

"No, they were little-bitty." Jackie stooped in the driveway and began heaping gravel in a dome-shaped pile. "Like this, only with pebbles from the creek. I'd put a stick in the top for a chimney and a flat piece of bark for the door." She rocked back on her heels to look up at Russell. "I built them for fairies. I told you it was dumb!"

"It's not dumb," Russell said. "You were a little kid with a great imagination. But, Jackie, how were the fairies supposed to get *in* the house if it was made of rocks? Shouldn't you have made the houses hollow?"

She collapsed with giggles, flattening the gravel hut. "I never thought of that!"

"Poor little fairies," Russell said with exaggerated sympathy. "They probably cracked their little noggins trying to use your solid rock houses. No wonder they never moved in. Promise me you won't be an architect when you grow up."

Jackie was laughing so hard she got the hiccups. "Sharon said I was too dumb to come in out of the rain. She's right!"

Russell pulled her to her feet. "Do you believe everything Sharon says?"

Jackie lounged companionably against the fender, copying Russell's stance. "Not any more. I used to chew my nails and one time Sharon told me it would make my appendix bust unless I stopped. Every time I got a pain in my side I thought it was my appendix."

"Sharon shouldn't have scared you like that," Russell commented.

Jackie shrugged. "She was always telling me stuff like that. I believed her because she's older." A snatch of dialog flashed through her brain. Forgetting she wanted to impress Russell, she said, "When I was little, Sharon would say, 'Who's prettier, me or you?' and I'd answer, 'You are, Sharon.' "

"I'm sure she was just teasing you."

"But Sharon *is* prettier. People say she looks like a young Elizabeth Taylor. She has an oval face. That's the perfect face shape to have, did you know that? You can wear any hairstyle if you have an oval face."

Russell's blue eyes twinkled with amusement. "Darn. I'm probably wearing my hair all wrong. What kind of face do you have?"

"A paper bag," she replied. At his surprised response, she explained. "In school sometimes the teacher would ask us to draw our own face. I always made mine like a paper bag. You know, with long straight sides and a round bottom and jiggy-jags at the top. That's what I look like."

Russell sighed. "Oh, Jackie."

"I hope you aren't going to hand me that old line about 'looks not being everything.'"

He laughed. "If I tell you something, will you believe me like you believe your sister? Because I'm older?"

Solemnly, she nodded.

"Don't sell yourself short. You're going to be a real heartbreaker some day," he said sincerely. "I guarantee it." He smiled and tweaked her nose. "And I think your paper-bag face is cute."

Jackie blushed and then she smiled back. Sharon really didn't deserve such a great guy, the way she was deceiving him.

Russell put his sunglasses on. "I'd better go," he said. "Oh, I nearly forgot."

"What?"

"You didn't take the five dollars Mr. Powell paid for distributing the fliers and William did."

She looked down at her bare feet. She couldn't very well take payment for something she hadn't done, now could she? William had earned his five dollars, but Jackie had chucked her fliers down a storm grate. "That's okay," she said. "I don't care."

"I care. You worked hard. I'd like to treat you."

Jackie held her breath. Was he going to ask her out — she hoped against hope — on a *date*?

"How would you like to go to the ice cream social at the Centreville firehouse tomorrow?" Russell asked.

"Oooh, I'd love it!" Then a thought hit her. "What about Sharon? Won't she be mad?"

116

Russell got into the car. "We'll take Sharon, too. Is that okay?"

It wasn't, but Jackie knew her mother wouldn't let her go to the ice cream social alone with an older boy. "I guess so," she said reluctantly.

"See you around one-thirty." Russell inserted the key into the ignition. "And Jackie, try to stop comparing yourself to your sister. You're a different person. You're going to do entirely different things than Sharon."

"Like what?" She leaned into the window, wishing he would kiss her good-bye.

"Anything you want. Swim the English channel, maybe." He put the car in gear and Jackie stepped back.

"Okay, but I have to learn to swim first!" she called as he left. When Russell's car was out of sight, Jackie did a little dance of joy in the driveway. She had a date! A real date with Russell Bass! Of course, Sharon would be along, but they'd make her sit in the back seat. Let Sharon be the little kid and Jackie the glamorous grown-up.

Dashing into the house, she ransacked her closet. What would she wear? All she had were skirts and tops, nothing really pretty. Then she remembered the new sundress Sharon had bought.

In Sharon's room, she shucked her shorts and T-shirt and slid into the white eyelet dress. The straps wouldn't stay up but the cool cotton felt delicious on her skin. Padding over to the mirror, Jackie saw with astonishment that she looked —

well, not exactly a heartbreaker, but not paper-bag-faced, either.

Standing so close to the mirror her breath fogged the surface, Jackie studied her reflection intensely, trying to see a glimmer of the face that would break hearts right and left in a few years.

At that moment Sharon came in. She stared at Jackie in her too-big sundress. "What are you doing?"

"Trying your dress on."

"I can see that." She tossed her purse on the bed. "Why?"

"I need something to wear tomorrow afternoon. Russell's taking me to the ice cream social at the firehouse," Jackie replied casually.

Sharon's jaw dropped. "You — what? Was Russell here?"

"He came by a little while ago. You weren't home. We talked and then he asked me to go to the social with him."

"Well, that's just great. What about me?"

"Oh, you're going, too. Russell said he'd be here at one-thirty to pick me — us — up." She flicked a strap up on her shoulder but it slipped off again.

Sharon went over to her vanity and began brushing her hair with agitated strokes. "What else did you and Russell talk about?" she asked stiffly.

"Nothing much," Jackie replied, deliberately vague. She twirled in Sharon's dress. "Russell says I'm going to be entirely different from you. And that one day I'm going to be a real heartbreaker. He guaranteed it!"

Sharon put the brush down with a clunk. "I have to get ready for work. Take my dress off."

Jackie obeyed. "Boy, are you grumpy. I pity the poor people who buy a pretzel from you."

When Sharon came home that night, Jackie was reading in bed. Sharon draped herself in the doorway and smiled, rather smugly, Jackie thought.

"What is it?" Jackie asked, wary as a salamander.

"I just want to let you know tomorrow's plans have been changed slightly. We're going to double date."

"A double date? Who are you going with?"

Sharon laughed indulgently. "No, no, little sister. You don't understand. It'll be me and Russell and you and William. Won't that be nice?"

"Over my dead body!" Jackie screamed, flinging her book down. "Russell asked *me*. I'm going with him. *You* can go with that nerdy brother of his."

Sharon flapped the hand weighed down with Russell's heavy class ring. "Don't be ridiculous. The adults will be together and the *children* will be together. That's the way it should be. Nighty-night!"

Jackie stood in her bed and yelled after her, "I'll get you for this, Sharon!"

The next day was hot and muggy, the kind of day best spent lying in the bathtub in a few inches of cool water. Humid or not, Jackie was determined to be dainty as a rose when Russell picked her up. Of course, Sharon hogged the bathroom for hours.

"It's my turn!" Jackie demanded, pounding on the bathroom door. "You've been in there long enough."

Sharon opened the door a sliver. Her hair was still damp from the shower. "I'll come out when I'm good and ready so stop all that racket."

But Jackie wasn't about to wait any longer. A cloud of shower steam billowed out as she forced her way in. "I know you," she said to Sharon. "You'll stay in here till it's almost time to go and make me late."

"Would I do that?" Sharon plugged in her razor, about to shave her legs. "It's too hot for both of us to be in here at the same time."

"Suffer a little." Jackie squeezed toothpaste on her brush and began brushing her teeth vigorously, just in case Sharon had actually told Russell all Jackie did was wet the toothbrush.

"You sound like you're scrubbing a battleship," said Sharon. "Do you have to make all that noise when you brush your teeth?"

"I want to make sure my breath is fresh," Jackie replied coyly, "in case Russell decides to kiss me."

"Well, you'll need to do more than brush your teeth," Sharon sniped. "It's a good thing the rescue squad will be there this afternoon."

"You should talk. The maple outside the window died when you opened your mouth just now." Trading insults was nothing new between Jackie and Sharon. But they had never used such catty tones with each other before.

Sharon finished shaving her legs and put the electric razor back in its case. She accidentally-on-purpose shoved Jackie to reach a bottle of lotion on the shelf, nearly causing Jackie to swallow her toothbrush.

Watching Sharon rub the fragrant cream on her legs, Jackie said, "You missed a patch of hair."

"Where?"

"Right there." Jackie pointed to her sister's big toe. "The hair's almost long enough to braid."

Sharon examined her foot. "I don't have any hair on my toes!"

"Gorilla feet, gorilla feet," Jackie chanted gleefully. "I wouldn't wear those sandals, if I were you."

"I do not have hairy toes," Sharon said in a clipped voice. "Excuse me." She left, pushing rudely past Jackie.

Jackie liberally applied the perfumy lotion to her own unshaved legs, then scampered to get dressed. The only appropriate outfit she had for the occasion was a white skirt with blue and green flowers and a white blouse. She'd used so much lotion, she had a little trouble keeping her sandals on her feet, but at last she was ready. She squished out to the living room.

Sharon was ready, too, standing by the picture window so she could be the first to spot Russell's car. She looked beautiful in her white eyelet dress, backdropped by the sheer priscilla curtains. Her delicate sandals laced around her ankles, like ballet slippers.

Jackie looked down at her own shoes. Her

sandals were old and buckled across her instep. If she had ribbon-tied sandals like Sharon's, she would glide gracefully as a swan instead of clumping around as if she were wearing wooden shoes.

"He's here," Sharon announced, turning from the window.

Jackie met her sister's eyes. Sharon was regarding her strangely, not as a grubby little sister horning in on her date, but — unbelievably — as a *rival*.

"Why are you staring at me like that?" she asked.

"I — I don't remember that skirt," Sharon said, not very convincingly.

"I've had it for ages. I don't buy clothes every five minutes like you do." Jackie smoothed the pockets over her hips. "You're not really looking at my skirt, are you?"

"If you think Russell is going to fall all over you because you reek of *my* lotion, you'd better think again," Sharon snapped.

"Well, *you* reek of it," Jackie countered. But suddenly Jackie knew, it wasn't the lotion or the skirt that had her sister rattled. Sharon was actually worried for the first time in her life because she had some competition!

Feeling a power she never knew she possessed, Jackie walked to the door, saying archly over her shoulder, "Coming, Sharon? It's not polite to keep the man waiting."

Chapter 12

The annual fund-raising event at the Centreville firehouse always attracted a big crowd. Pots of pink geraniums made a bright splash of color against the brick retaining wall. Japanese lanterns outlined the eating area, where chairs had been grouped under yellow-striped umbrellas. Pink and yellow plastic cloths covered the ice cream tables. The grills of the fire engines and the ambulances were decorated with big yellow bows. Even Sparky the fire dog sported a festive yellow ribbon.

"Suppose there's a fire," William remarked as soon as he stepped from Russell's car. "Then what?"

"Cheery thought," Jackie said. "I bet you're a barrel of laughs at a funeral." She was in a bad mood because she'd tried to beat Sharon to the front seat so she could sit next to Russell, but her sister had elbowed her out of the way. Jackie sat squashed against the window in the back seat, as far away from William as she could get.

"I've only been to one funeral," William said earnestly. "My great-aunt Mary's. She looked terrible, all — "

"William!" Russell interrupted. "Move it so I can pay for our tickets."

"Hers, too?" William indicated Jackie with a jerk of his thumb. Jackie wanted to crawl under the nearest ladder truck.

A ticket entitled them to five dishes of home-made ice cream. If they wanted more, they could purchase another ticket. Jackie couldn't imagine eating five dishes of ice cream, let alone ten. The women from the Ladies Auxiliary also provided iced tea, lemonade, and plain sugar cookies.

Jackie's mood softened when she saw couples strolling arm and arm around the grounds, admiring the flowers. In this romantic setting, Russell would put his arm around her waist and whisper sweet nothings in her ear —

"What kind do you want first?" William bellowed, bringing Jackie crashing down to earth.

"What kind what?"

"*Ice* cream. What do you think we're *here* for?"

It was then she noticed that Russell wasn't even walking with her. Sharon hung possessively on to his hand, steering him away from the tables to a bench under a huge lilac bush.

"Vanilla," she replied, distracted.

William pulled a face. "Vanilla? Yuck. I want black raspberry."

"All right. I'll have that, too." Jackie sat down

on one of the folding chairs and smoothed her skirt. Maybe Russell would only stay with Sharon for a minute, before leaving her to spend the rest of the afternoon with Jackie —

"You certainly don't expect *me* to carry two bowls, do you?" William blasted her thoughts again. "Are your legs broke?"

"No," she said, looking anxiously back at the bench. Russell seemed very content talking with her sister. How would she ever survive an afternoon with this dreadful boy?

They walked over to the table where a lady dipped ice cream into plastic dishes. Ever gracious, William cut in front of Jackie so he could be served first. Before Jackie had even thanked the lady who scooped her ice cream, William had gobbled his and was ready for bowl number two.

"Come on!" William hustled Jackie over to the next table. "I want to get the butter almond before it's all gone."

Jackie gulped a spoonful of ice cream so fast, a sharp pain knifed her temple. Homemade ice cream was a lot colder than store-bought. "I can't eat any faster!"

William stood on tiptoe to peer into the wooden bucket. "There's only a little bit left," he moaned, then counted the people in line ahead of him in a not-very-subtle voice.

"For Pete's sake, there are fifteen tables," Jackie said, shrinking with humiliation.

"But they might run out before it's our turn!" William jostled the person directly in front of him until the man left the line, scowling at William. "Here's yours." William thrust the dish of butter almond at Jackie, who hadn't finished her first bowl.

"I can't eat two dishes at once," she protested. "Let's go sit down."

"I'll eat yours," he said. "We can't waste time sitting down. We still have thirteen more tables to hit."

Russell and Sharon meandered into view again. They were sharing a bowl of chocolate ice cream. Russell fed Sharon a spoonful, then Sharon fed Russell some. Jackie's throat ached just watching them. *She* should be having a romantic interlude with Russell, instead of an ice cream rampage with an eleven-year-old maniac. William wouldn't even slow down, she was certain, until they had sampled every single flavor.

While they were waiting in line at the third table, William scarfed Jackie's dish of butter almond. Then he bolted a scoop of rocky road with such zest, Jackie wondered where he was putting it. He finished her portion of rocky road and was scooping out the next flavor when Jackie said bluntly, "If you want to keep pigging out, you can. I'll be over there."

She went over to the chairs and sat down. Let that idiot carry on his ice cream marathon by himself, she thought. With dismay, she noticed a glob of chocolate on her skirt. She scrubbed the stain with a paper napkin, but only smeared it worse. It was William's fault, making her gallop from table to table.

Sharon and Russell came over.

"Hey there, Cupcake. How're you doing?" Russell asked Jackie.

"Fine," she replied, but her voice didn't carry much conviction.

Russell scanned the crowd. "Where's William?"

"In line for banana. If he doesn't get it, he says he's going to sue."

Russell laughed. "Somebody else said the banana is great. Want some, Sharon?"

She smiled up at him. "No, thanks. I've had enough."

Jackie stared at her sister. Four little spoonfuls of chocolate ice cream filled her up? Ordinarily, Sharon could consume a washing tub of ice cream and still have room for Jackie's.

"I'll be right back," Russell told her.

When he was gone, Sharon asked archly, "How's it going with William?"

"How do you *think* I'm doing with a little twerp only interested in gorging on ice cream? You owe me, Sharon, but good."

"Why, whatever do you mean?" Sharon sounded like she was auditioning for the part of Amy March in *Little Women*.

"You know exactly what I mean! You're deliberately keeping Russell away from me. This is *my* date — he asked me. You're monopolizing all his time."

Sharon stood up. "I can monopolize Russell's time. He's *my* boyfriend."

Russell came back with a dish of banana ice cream for himself and a plate of sugar cookies for Sharon and Jackie. "William's still chowing down. That kid really loves ice cream."

"He certainly gets his money's worth," Sharon said. "Look, the fire chief is letting people climb up on the engine. Can we go over?"

"Sure, you can even ring the bell. Can I finish this first? It's really good." Russell shoveled a big spoonful of ice cream.

"You don't want all that fattening stuff. Let's get a little exercise." Sharon dragged Russell to the fire engines, laughing.

Thoroughly provoked, Jackie wondered if she could murder her sister with all these witnesses. Sharon wouldn't let Russell spend two seconds with her!

William staggered over to the chairs and collapsed with a groan. "My stomach hurts!"

"It ought to. You ate five bowls plus finished three of mine." Jackie didn't feel the slightest bit sorry for the little glutton. "You'll probably be sick as a dog later. All those flavors churning around . . . rocky road, black raspberry, banana — "

William quickly took a sip of Sharon's ice water. "Hey, people are climbing on the fire engine."

"That's for babies," Jackie sniffed.

"Your sister is doing it. She's no baby," William said admiringly.

Sharon certainly didn't look like a baby as Russell lifted her into the high seat. Her skirt rose briefly above her knees, giving everyone a glimpse of her long legs. People smiled at the beautiful girl waving from the cab of the fire engine.

Jackie felt lumpish and dowdy in her flowered skirt with the chocolate stain. She knew her face was red from the sun and the humidity had made her hair straggly.

"Your sister's pretty," William said, implying that not only was Jackie the direct opposite, but that it was hard to believe Sharon and Jackie were from the same family.

" 'Looks aren't everything,' " Jackie quoted piously.

"I guess they aren't when you don't have them," William said, infuriating Jackie even more. "My brother is crazy about your sister. That's all he talks about at home. Sharon this and Sharon that. I bet they get married."

"Sharon has no intention of marrying your brother," Jackie said scathingly, feeling vengeful. Sharon had spoiled her whole afternoon.

William jeered, "What are you, jealous?"

"Certainly not," Jackie said haughtily. "Anybody can see my sister is making a fool out of your brother."

He stared at her. "What do you mean?"

"Sharon's going with a guy named Mick. They've been dating since Thanksgiving," she said recklessly. "She doesn't care about your brother. The only reason she's going out with him is because she wanted a summer romance. She told me so herself. When September comes, it'll be bye-bye Russell."

"I don't believe it!"

"I don't care what you believe. It's the truth."
And time Russell knew it, too. William had an
incredibly big mouth — he'd tell his brother before the day was over. And her sister, the traitor,
would be minus one boyfriend.

Jackie loved to eat lima beans, but she de-
spised shelling them. The hulls were so tough
they made her fingers sore and the reward for
tearing one open was paltry, two or three flat
beans.

"Is this enough?" she asked, tilting her pan
so her mother could see how many she had
shelled.

"Not quite," Mrs. Howard said, but then she'd
been saying that for the last hour, ever since she
decided to freeze lima beans.

"I hate this job," Jackie grumbled. "I hate this
worse than anything in the world."

"I'm not too crazy about it myself," her mother
admitted. "But think how good succotash will
taste this winter when the snow is flying. And
vegetable soup."

"I don't like vegetable soup." Jackie dug open
a tough pod with a ragged thumbnail. "I like
that soup you make in a cup with hot water."

Sharon hobbled into the kitchen with cotton
pads wedged between each toe.

"What is wrong with your feet?" Mrs. Howard
asked with alarm.

"Nothing." Sharon plucked a lima bean out
of Jackie's pan and ate it raw. "I just gave myself
a pedicure."

130

"Using my new polish," Mrs. Howard observed. "Who is it this afternoon?"

"Mick." Sharon sat down in her father's chair. "We're going to Glen Echo."

Mrs. Howard looked up from the steaming kettle. "That wild place. I don't like you going there, Sharon."

"It's not wild. Just because a place has a roller coaster, you assume it's dangerous. Anyway, we won't be there long because I want to try to see Russell before work."

"Have you ever heard of burning the candle at both ends?"

Sharon dropped a bean to Felix. The cat batted it with his paw, like a hockey puck. "I'm just exercising my independence."

Mrs. Howard came over to check Jackie's progress. "That's enough. Thanks, Jackie." To Sharon she said, "You do what you want. You always have. But one of these days you'll find out that doing what you want isn't necessarily the right thing, like stringing two boys along."

Sharon went off like a Roman candle, straight up and sputtering. "You don't understand me! I'll be glad when I'm old enough to leave home."

"So will I," said Jackie. Sharon glared at her. "While you're out with Mick, I think I'll call up Russell."

"No, you won't," Sharon said.

"I can if I want to. You were the one who told me to make lots of calls. I'm just trying to get over my phone shyness."

Mrs. Howard dumped the beans Jackie shelled

131

into the kettle. "Why can't Jackie call Russell? He's her friend."

"Russell has better things to do than talk to a little kid," Sharon snapped.

"I'm not a little kid," Jackie contradicted.

"No, she's not." Amazingly, her mother sided with her. "Jackie's thirteen. She's growing up."

"Yeah, Sharon," Jackie needled. "I'm growing up. I bet your new sundress will fit me in a week or so."

"Oh, shut up." Sharon stamped out of the room, leaving wads of cotton puffs in her wake.

Freed from chores, Jackie went outdoors. Twigs and limbs blown by the previous night's thunderstorm littered the yard. On an impulse, Jackie headed for the creek. She hadn't been there since the day of her picnic.

Jackie reached the top of the hill where the Civil War fence zigzagged along the property boundary. The fence had actually been built before the Civil War, over a hundred years before. In a few places, the oak rails had tumbled like surrendered muskets, but most of the fence remained standing. The fence had been constructed without nails; poles were propped in a teepee design and the rails were laid between the poles.

The memory of Russell helping Sharon over the fence on the day of her picnic flitted through Jackie's mind. She kicked at the rail nearest her. The ancient oak board fell much easier than she thought it would, taking the bottom rail with it. No longer supported by the rails, the poles toppled. Where there had been an unbroken line, there was now a gaping hole, for the first time in more than a hundred years.

Horrified at what she had done, she tried to heft the oak rail back into place, but it was like reassembling a house of pick-up-sticks. The poles kept sliding and the rail was too ungainly for one person to handle. Another part of the woods ruined, just like the creek. This was Sharon's fault, too, indirectly.

William Bass had probably blabbed to his brother about how Sharon was only using him for a summer fling. Sharon will be in for a shock when she sees Russell later this evening, thinking everything was rosy. About time her sister got her just desserts.

Jackie left the oak rail lying in the drifted leaves and went back home.

Chapter 13

Jackie counted a total of five cars in the customer parking lot. Business was definitely not booming at Old Virginia City.

"Mama said I could stay all evening," she told her father as he let her and Sharon out. As they passed through the gate, Jackie thought Mr. Powell, the owner, looked very down in the mouth.

Sharon took over the refreshment booth, exchanging a few comments with the girl who ran it during the afternoon. "Looks like Russell's idea isn't working," she remarked to Jackie. "A couple of people came for the free pony ride, but not enough to make a difference."

"I'm going to see Russell," Jackie said. She was antsy, nervously waiting for the events she'd set in motion at the ice cream social to explode.

Sharon poured herself a Coke. "Tell him to meet me during his break."

The whole park seemed to be on a break, there were so few people around.

Russell was grooming Cookie. He didn't greet her with his usual "Hey there, Cupcake." Instead he asked tonelessly, "Is your sister here?"

"She's up at her booth," Jackie replied. William must have tattled! Russell looked terrible, as if he hadn't slept in weeks. "So, what's new?" she said, anxious for his response. Here was his chance to confess what a fool he'd been, falling for shallow beauty while he let the one girl in his life slip through his fingers.

Without replying, Russell turned away from her to examine the pony's hoof.

Sensing he wasn't in the mood for chit-chat, Jackie wandered back up to her sister's booth.

Sharon checked her watch. "Russell's break is almost over. Is he busy down there?"

"Not really," Jackie said.

"I wonder why he hasn't come up to see me? I didn't see him earlier."

Because he's finally learned the truth about you, Jackie refrained from saying.

Sharon looked down the deserted concourse. "What's keeping him?"

"He's not a trained pony," Jackie said, annoyed at her sister's possessiveness.

"What's that supposed to mean?"

"Nothing." Jackie picked at a crust of mustard dried on the counter.

Sharon raised the bar to her booth. "I'm going down there."

135

"Your break isn't for another half hour," Jackie said.

But Sharon was already heading down the concourse. "I don't care. I have to find out what's up with Russell."

Jackie lingered a few minutes, then, not wanting to miss the fireworks, she ran down to the pony ride. The chain anchored across the entrance told her Russell had finally taken his break.

Hearing voices behind the barn, Jackie followed the fence around back, where she found her sister and Russell. She couldn't catch actual words but it was apparent they were arguing. Russell's jaw was like granite. Sharon seemed to be pleading with him. At last, tearfully, Sharon tugged the class ring off her finger and gave it to him. She wheeled and left the pony yard, glancing up to see Jackie hanging on the fence.

Her sister's face was tear-streaked. "Well," Sharon said, still crying. "I suppose you heard. Probably everybody in Old Virginia City heard."

Jackie swallowed. "No, I didn't. I mean, I could tell you guys were fighting, but I don't know what about."

They walked a short distance until they were in a fairly private area of the park, at the end of the "town."

Sharon sagged against the rough-board wall of the Post Office and let the tears flow. "Russell broke up with me," she sobbed. "He said he knew about Mick! He called me a two-timer and that I was just stringing him along. Who could have told him about Mick?"

"Uh — maybe he ran into Mick," Jackie stammered. "He comes to the park sometimes, you know." Her palms were slick with perspiration. Sharon was no dummy. Any second now she'd grasp the truth . . . and then clobber the stool pigeon who started the whole thing.

"Mick doesn't have a clue about Russell. I've been very careful to keep them separated. Somebody told Russ — " She broke off to stare at Jackie. "It was you!" she accused, fury darkening her brown eyes. "You did it!"

Jackie took a step backward. "I didn't! It's a lie!"

"Don't you stand there flat-footed and tell me about lying, Jacqueline Howard," Sharon said through clenched teeth. "Who *else* could have told Russell?"

"His brother!"

"What?"

"It wasn't me," Jackie said. "It was William. *He* told Russell."

"And who told William?" Sharon grilled. "You, that's who. Don't try to cover up, Jackie. I know you did it."

Jackie couldn't wiggle out of this one. Sharon would keep her in Old Virginia City until they were both old and gray. "It was at the ice cream social," she confessed, as her whole life — brief as it was — passed before her eyes. "I was miserable because you ruined my date with Russell. And then William started telling me how crazy Russell was about you. He said you and Russell would probably get married some day, and I told him you were going with another guy."

"Marriage! Russell was getting awfully serious," Sharon said, almost to herself. But then her attention swung back to Jackie. "You couldn't keep your big mouth shut, could you?"

"I didn't mean for you guys to break up," Jackie said weakly.

"Oh, yes, you did. You knew exactly what you were doing. You couldn't stand it that Russell and I were dating so you broke us up. You make me sick, Jackie Howard."

Something within Jackie snapped. It was as though all the niggling little changes that had been shifting for weeks now surged together in a single tidal wave. "You make me just as sick, Sharon Howard! Sicker! You stole Russell from me, and you got just what you deserved!"

"How could I steal what wasn't yours? This is the thanks I get for trying to help you this summer. And you have the nerve to call *me* a traitor."

Jackie didn't flinch from her sister's harsh accusations. "You are! The Sister Rebellion was *my* idea, but once you got what you wanted, you couldn't care less about helping me. You're the one who's holding me back, not Mama. Everywhere I go — everything I do — you're there first. I never have a chance as long as you're around. You think you'll be glad when you leave home? Well, I'll be double-glad! Triple-glad!"

Sharon didn't say anything for several wrenching seconds, shocked by Jackie's outburst. Jackie was rather surprised herself. And then she thought, what a strange place to have a showdown with Sharon, in the middle of a phony wild west town. This whole summer had been as false as the facade of Old Virginia City, promising everything but delivering nothing.

"I hope you're satisfied," Sharon said at last. "Your little scheme worked. Russell never wants to see me again."

Jackie started to reply, but a shout from the other end of the park interrupted her. "Did that guy just yell fire?"

"I see smoke coming from the concession area!" Sharon shrieked. "I hope Buddy's all right!"

But people were running toward the refreshment stand, not the shooting gallery. As they drew closer, Jackie could see flames licking the red-striped awning of Sharon's booth. Buddy and some other men were connecting hoses to a spigot outside the restaurant.

Sharon blanched. "Oh, my gosh, it's my stand! My booth is on fire!"

"Sharon!" Jackie cried as her sister raced into the crowd. She dashed after her, but a man in a cowboy suit grabbed her arm.

"Stay out of the way, young lady," Mr. Powell ordered.

"But the fire . . . my sister!"

"There's nothing to be scared of. Just a little accident. We'll have it under control in no time." Releasing her, Mr. Powell joined the men holding the hose. One of the firefighters was Russell. When the hose was long enough to reach the booth, he handed the nozzle to Buddy and signaled that the water be turned on. Buddy aimed the hose at the burning awning. The canvas crackled as water met flames.

Jackie located Sharon standing off to one side. "Mr. Powell said it's not as bad as it looks," she told her. "They almost have it out."

"I should have been there," Sharon said, her eyes riveted to the scene before her. "It's all my fault."

Engine Company Number 17 from Centreville roared into the parking lot just then. She and Sharon got pushed back even farther from the action as firemen unreeled hoses and proceeded to extinguish the blaze. When the smoke cleared, Jackie noted that only the awning was completely scorched. The booth itself was charred but intact.

Buddy Myers came over and put his arm around Sharon. "It's not so bad, really. Not nearly as much damage as there could have been."

Sharon sniffed, on the verge of tears again. "It's all my fault, Buddy. I went on my break without having somebody relieve me. Do they know what started the fire? Was it the pretzel oven?"

"Naw. Mr. Powell thinks some guy threw a cigarette in the trash can. That's where it started, not in the booth."

Sharon buried her face in her hands. "He's going to fire me. I just know it."

"Sharon, it could have happened to any one of us," said Buddy. "Mr. Powell won't blame you. He's just glad nobody got hurt."

But Sharon would not be consoled. "It's still my fault. If I'd been there like I was supposed to . . . I should quit. Save Mr. Powell the trouble."

Jackie watched Russell walk by. If the fire was Sharon's fault, then it was partly his, too. Then it dawned on her that the reason Sharon left her booth in the first place was because Russell was mad at her. And who was responsible for the fight between Russell and her sister? *Jackie* was to blame, not Sharon. If anybody should quit, it ought to be Jackie. But she didn't have a job or a boyfriend. She had nothing to lose. Maybe that was why she felt so empty inside.

When their parents learned about the fire, they were predictably upset. Mrs. Howard said she didn't want Sharon going back to such a dangerous job, that she was afraid all along something would happen and now it had.

"I don't want to talk about this tonight," Sharon told them wearily. "I have to see Mr. Powell tomorrow afternoon. He'll probably let me go, and you'll get your wish." She went into her room without a word to Jackie.

In her own room, Jackie could hear her sister banging and thumping through the wall that separated their rooms. What was Sharon doing in there, packing to move? Curious, Jackie knocked once on her sister's door and went in.

Everything in the universe was on the floor. Clothes, books, records, Sharon's drill team uniform, papers, socks, Felix's pink rubber mouse, blankets, magazines, and pillows. In the center of the chaos, Sharon stripped her bed. More junk flew out of the covers like confetti.

"What are you doing?" Jackie asked.

"What does it look like?" Sharon replied tightly. "I'm cleaning my room."

"But it's after eleven!"

"I don't care if it's three in the morning. I can't sleep in this hogpen another night." She yanked the bottom sheet which jerked free from the mattress in a hurricane of candy wrappers, anklets, wadded-up Kleenex, and what appeared to be an entire bottle of those tiny multi-colored dots used to decorate cakes. Pink, green, and blue pellets bounced like beebees.

"Need some help?" Jackie offered.

Sharon's voice was brittle. "No, thanks. You've helped me enough for one night."

Jackie knelt to retrieve the colored pellets rolling in all directions. "You'll have to vacuum these up."

Sharon stuffed sheets into a mammoth heap of dirty laundry. "If I want your advice I'll ask for it."

Jackie paused, multi-colored dots sticking to her fingers. She wanted to tell Sharon she was sorry, but the incident at Old Virginia City was too big to dismiss with a couple of words. What she wanted, she supposed, was Sharon to forgive her. But of course, that was expecting too much.

"Well . . . I heard the noise in here, and I came in to see what you were doing," Jackie said simply.

"Now you know. Now you know everything

so you ought to be happy." Sharon sounded like she was going to cry again.

Jackie went back to her own room and got into bed. She leaned her elbows on the windowsill and stared out into the sultry night. Crickets chirruped, a sign that summer was almost over. A firefly blinked in the August lily beneath her window. Jackie tried to follow the bug's path, secret and unlit. When the firefly flashed again, she discovered she'd been looking in the wrong place.

The distant woods were like black cutouts against a slightly lighter background. She tried to find the poodle and the lady in the treetops but couldn't. Where were her old familiar friends? The horizon was different now, shapeless.

Maybe the storm that night had altered the treeline, created a new pattern. Jackie stared until her eyes watered, searching for the figures in the trees. But she couldn't see anything.

Maybe, she mused, it would be a while before the new pattern revealed itself to her, before the changes made sense.

Chapter 14

Sharon did lose her job, but not because of the fire. Business at Old Virginia City had been declining steadily since opening day. Half the employees were laid off, not just Sharon. The rest were staying on until Labor Day. After that, the park would shut down until Mr. Powell, the saddest cowboy in the East, found a buyer.

Sharon continued dating Mick Rowe as if nothing had happened. They went to the movies and to Lake Fairfax. Russell Bass never called or dropped by. Jackie missed him, and she knew Sharon did, too.

Jackie's final days of summer were filled helping her mother can the bounty of vegetables from the garden. More like an invasion, Jackie thought. Tomatoes early in July were a treat, earthy-tasting and juicy, but tomatoes in August were a bore. Pails of them, picked by Mr. Howard before he left for work, appeared on the porch every morning for Jackie to wash. What Mrs. Howard didn't can, they gave away or foisted on people. Even the gas meter reader couldn't leave without a bag. And still the tomatoes kept coming.

The last Saturday in August was reserved for school shopping, which usually meant a trip to the closest town, Manassas. But this year they were going to Clarendon, a real outing. Jackie and Sharon would be on their own in the big department stores, while their parents visited friends in nearby Arlington.

"Remember the time we came through Seven Corners and the car died?" Mr. Howard asked, as they idled at a stoplight.

"Oh, Daddy," Jackie said from the back seat. "Do you have to bring that up again?"

"How many people have their cars quit on them in the worst intersection in Virginia?" He pointed to the fateful spot where seven major roads met in a junction of arrows and ramps. "Who would have dreamed that on the hottest day of the year, Jackie would have poured dirt in the gas tank before we started out?"

Mrs. Howard's shoulders shook with suppressed laughter. "She was only five."

Jackie felt compelled to defend herself, which she had to do every time they drove through Seven Corners. "I saw this little door on the side of the car and it looked like a neat place to put things. So I unscrewed the cap and put in a couple of handfuls of dirt from the driveway in it. I didn't mean to ruin the car."

The light changed. Mr. Howard advanced into the intersection, embellishing the story. "We got right about here, and the car just conked out. I looked under the hood, but couldn't see a thing. Finally I had it towed to the garage over there." Everyone stared at the garage, a nondescript building vital to their family history, like tourists gawking at the White House.

"Clogged gas line," Mr. Howard repeated the mechanic's diagnosis mournfully. "The car was a goner. I had to junk it."

"And we had to buy a new one," Mrs. Howard added. "An expense we really couldn't afford at the time. We'd just moved from Manassas to the new house, remember? But we managed. Somehow we've always managed, haven't we?" She smiled at her husband.

"My red Ford convertible. My favorite car." Mr. Howard sighed. "Oh, well, we needed a more sensible car with the girls getting bigger."

Jackie glanced over at Sharon. This was the perfect opportunity for her sister to get in a good dig. Ruining an entire car was by far the worst thing anybody in the family had ever done, worse than the time Sharon fell through the living room ceiling in a friend's house. How many other five-year-olds wrecked the family car? But Sharon fiddled with the clasp on her purse, contributing nothing to the conversation.

Things between Jackie and Sharon had been strained since that awful day at Old Virginia City. They didn't fight, but they weren't exactly on sisterly terms either.

Mr. Howard pulled up at the entrance to

Hecht's department store. "We'll meet you here in two hours," he said.

"If you get hungry, go have a sandwich in Murphy's," Mrs. Howard instructed.

"Yes, Mother," Sharon replied, rolling her eyes at Jackie.

Jackie agreed. As if they didn't have enough sense to eat when they were hungry! Next their mother would tell them to be sure and take a nap if they got tired.

Inside the store, Sharon said, businesslike, "I'm going to the Misses section. I'll meet you here under the clock in an hour."

Jackie cruised the perfume counter, spraying herself with the testers until the saleslady gave her a dirty look. She took the escalator up to the Junior department.

There were racks of dresses and skirts and sweaters, back to school clothes in fall colors. Even though it was still sweltering, summer was officially over. Her friend Natalie would be back from Seattle. She'd probably call Jackie this weekend to tell her about her great summer. And what would Jackie say she had done? Washed tomatoes and slapped gnats.

She went over to the record department and bought the album she'd been trying to win on WPGC most of the summer. Her mother paid her a twenty-five dollar bonus for helping in the garden, in addition to her regular allowance. Money usually burned a hole in her pocket, but Jackie couldn't think of anything else to buy. Even though the hour wasn't up, she rode the escalator down to the Misses department.

147

She found Sharon pirouetting before the three-way mirror in a white net gown. The dress had spaghetti straps, tiny pearls sewn around the neckline, and a full tiered skirt. Her sister looked beautiful.

"It's perfect for you," Jackie breathed, coming up behind her to touch the fragile fabric.

"Do you really think so?" Sharon sashayed back and forth, making the skirt swish around her ankles. "I'd love to buy it, but where would I wear it?"

"Your senior prom," Jackie replied promptly. "You'll need a new dress for that."

Sharon tugged the price into view. Her face fell. "I don't have enough money."

"You could lay it away," Jackie suggested.

Sharon estimated the percentage she'd have to put down, then shook her head. "No, I can't. I spent most of my money on other stuff. I didn't see this dress until a few minutes ago. Oh, well. Maybe it'll still be here when Mom comes back to do her Christmas shopping."

"But it might be gone."

Sharon shrugged. "It's the chance I'll have to take. There'll be other dresses." She poufed the skirt, admiring her reflection with a wistful smile.

Jackie made a quick decision. True, her sister seemed to have everything, beauty, a boyfriend, and certainly plenty of clothes. But this dress really *was* made for Sharon. She ought to have it. And Jackie had money to lend her.

"I still have twenty dollars," Jackie said hesitantly. "If that's enough, I'll loan it to you."

"Would you?" Sharon's face lit up for the first time in days. "That'd be terrific! I'll pay you back as soon as I can." She gave Jackie a hug. "This is so great. You know what? I think we need to talk. I'll take care of my dress first and then we can go get a Coke." She skipped off to the dressing room.

Jackie let out a pent-up sigh of relief. At last she and her sister were going to clear the air!

When the white gown was safely laid away in Sharon's name, the girls went downstairs to the coffee shop for a soda. They sat uneasily across from each other, alone for the first time since the night of the fire.

Sharon made rings on the table with the wet bottom of her glass. "Well, school starts next week. Summer's over."

"So's the Sister Rebellion," said Jackie.

Sharon laughed shortly. "Our summer of independence. What a joke!"

"You made out all right. You got a job, more boys than you could handle. . . ." Jackie paused. They had not mentioned Russell since the night of the fire. "You even drove the car. You're out in the world now." But I'm still stuck at home, she thought.

"No, I'm not," Sharon disagreed, shaking her head ruefully. "I blew it but good this summer."

"What are you talking about?"

"All that business Mom was telling me, about how you can't do as you please and never face the consequences. Well, much as I hate to admit it, she was right." Sharon stared at the three linked circles she'd just made with her glass. "I thought I was hot stuff this summer, with my job and two guys."

Jackie didn't understand what her sister was getting at. "But you *were* hot stuff. I mean, you did all those things."

When Sharon looked at her, Jackie read misery in her sister's eyes. "Independence isn't what it's cracked up to be, Jackie. Like that job. It was mostly work, taking other people's guff while you waited on them. And I didn't act responsibly, leaving my booth when I wasn't supposed to. But the worst part was hurting Russell."

Jackie squirmed with guilt. "I was the one who made him mad."

"All you did was speed things up. It was bound to happen anyway. I doubt we would have lasted till September."

"But I thought you liked Russell."Jackie was confused.

"I did, but not as much as he liked me. At the ice cream social, he was talking about maybe getting me a promise ring. You know, one of those teeny pre-engagement diamonds? I wasn't ready to be that committed. Deep down inside I think I really *was* having a summer romance with Russell, but I didn't want to give him up." Sharon paused. "And there was something else."

"What?"

"I was jealous . . . of you."

Jackie wondered if her sister was crazy from the heat. "*You* were jealous of *me*? I don't believe it."

"It's true," Sharon said with a small smile.

"Russell liked you a lot. He thought you were adorable. He told me so. Several times."

"Only because I was your little sister."

"No," Sharon stated. "He liked you because you're cute and funny. You *are* thirteen. Old enough for boys, even an older boy like Russell, to notice. I only noticed myself this summer."

Jackie didn't say anything, thinking about the petty way she instigated the break-up between her sister and Russell and caused the fire at Sharon's booth. She hadn't acted very responsibly, either. Life was a lot like knocking the Civil War fence down, she thought. Something was in place a long time until someone like her came along and kicked at it, changing the order forever.

"At least you tried," Jackie said. "I didn't do anything this summer except cause trouble because I was jealous. You know what I did? The day we stuffed mailboxes, I threw my fliers down the sewer."

Sharon laughed. "I wish I had thought of that! I wanted to throw mine away, too, but Russell was with me the whole time." At the mention of his name, the girls were silent a moment.

"I'm still a bigger failure than you are," Jackie said morosely.

"Are you kidding?" Sharon raised her eyebrows. "You took over for me in the garden and didn't complain once. That takes — fortitude. You're not nearly as shy as you were," Sharon went on. "You don't have to worry about Mom and Dad holding you back anymore. I don't think *any*body could hold you back."

"Really?" A warm feeling of pleasure, like hot chocolate on a chilly winter afternoon, flowed through Jackie.

"Really," her sister said. And she meant it.

At home, Sharon spread her purchases on her bed while Jackie played her new album on Sharon's stereo. Mrs. Howard came in with the mail. She wasn't too pleased that Jackie had lent most of her school-shopping money to her sister for a prom dress, but Jackie insisted she'd wanted to do it.

"I take full responsibility for my actions," Jackie said stoutly.

"Is that right? Well, it'll be the first time for either of you girls." But her mother said it in such a way Jackie knew she was only kidding. "Sharon," Mrs. Howard added, "I can actually walk in this room."

"I thought I'd try being neat for a change," said Sharon.

"Don't change too fast. I won't be able to stand it."

"Oh, Mom." Sharon spoke with fond indulgence, as if their mother were an old caretaker Sharon had to let go. "You just have to face it . . . Jackie and I are growing up. One day we'll be gone."

Mrs. Howard pretended to cry. "You girls are going off and leaving your poor mother?"

"Don't worry, Mama," Jackie said, afraid her mother would really start crying. "I'll be around for a while."

Sharon snipped the price tag from a sweater

with a pair of cuticle scissors. "Jackie might leave when she's forty or so."

"That'll be fine with your father and me," Mrs. Howard told Jackie.

"Well — " Jackie wasn't planning to leave home after next year like Sharon, but she didn't think she'd stick around quite that long.

Mrs. Howard laughed. "You won't hurt our feelings if you decide to fly away from the nest before then." She riffled through the mail. "Postcard for you, Jackie."

"For me?" Jackie took the card. "It must be from Natalie."

"Pretty beach picture," Mrs. Howard remarked on her way out.

Jackie flipped the card over, hardly looking at the photograph on the front. "She promised she'd write the first week she got there, and all I got was a crummy postcard — " She stopped. The printing on the back was too neat to be Natalie's.

Sharon was watching her face. "It's not from Natalie."

"No, it's from Russell," Jackie gasped.

"Russell? Are you sure it's for you?" Sharon held a blouse in one hand and a hanger in the other, ready to drop both in case Jackie had made a mistake.

Jackie read the address out loud. " 'Miss Jacqueline Howard.' That's me."

"What does he *say*?"

"Well, he says . . ." Her voice trailed off. Suddenly Jackie didn't want to share the postcard with her sister. Russell had written "Hey there, Cupcake" at the beginning of the message section. Jackie could almost hear him calling her that special nickname.

"Did you go to sleep or something?" Sharon pressed. "I asked you what he said."

"Nothing much," Jackie hedged. "Just that he's at Rehoboth Beach, and he thought of me when he saw this card."

What Russell had actually written was: "Hey there, Cupcake. How are you doing? Decided to go with my buddies to catch the last rays before it's back to the grind. When I saw this card, I thought of you. It isn't exactly the English Channel, but you know what I mean. Take care. Russ."

Staring at the ocean scene on the front of the postcard, Jackie remembered their talk in the driveway, leaning against Russell's car. He'd told her to stop comparing herself to Sharon, that she was a different person, not a smaller, plainer version of her sister. Her life would be different from Sharon's. According to Russell, the possibilities were limitless, up to and including swimming the English Channel!

Her heart lifted, Jackie offered the postcard to her sister. "Want to read it?"

Sharon considered. "No, thanks. It's your private personal mail. Obviously Russell doesn't mention me. And why should he? After all, he fell for you first. He'll remember you the longest."

Jackie was glad she could keep one little part of her summer a secret. The postcard was the only reminder of her first love, that and her

154

memories. "I think he'll remember us both," she said.

Sharon laughed. "The devastating Howard sisters." She finished hanging her new clothes in her closet. "Hey, know what I want to do?"

"What?"

"Let's go outside and sit on the quilt like we used to. We haven't done that all summer."

Jackie glanced out the window, hugging her postcard. The garden was surrendering to the jungly weeds, now that most of the vegetables had been harvested. Early twilight sketched long violet shadows across the yard.

Suddenly Jackie realized that the wonderful thing she'd been waiting for had been happening all along, like the gradual progression from summer to fall. She was changing, just as the landscape was changing, enough to make an older guy like Russell Bass notice.

Her days *weren't* always going to be the same, not as long as there were different seasons. And not as long as her sister was around to keep life interesting. Sure, Sharon was light-years ahead of her, but Jackie was finally catching up.

Sharon waited at the door. "You coming?"

"Yes," said Jackie, and went to get the quilt from the linen closet.

About the Author

CANDICE FARRIS RANSOM, born July 10, 1952, is a younger sister. Many of her stories, including the popular Kobie books, *Going on Twelve*, *Thirteen*, *Fourteen and Holding*, and *Fifteen at Last* are based on her own experiences growing up. Ms. Ransom says, "My brain stops at about age fifteen. I'm a grown-up by default."

Raised in Centreville, Virginia, Ms. Ransom still makes her home there with her husband, Frank, and one cat.